LewiSF

Monster Stories

This book of monster stories belongs to

Lewis Fitzgerald

Lewiz FF

Monster Stories

Written by
Andy Charman, Beatrice Phillpotts, Caroline Repchuk,
Louisa Somerville and Christine Tagg

Illustrated by
Diana Catchpole, Robin Edmonds, Chris Forsey
and Claire Mumford

This is a Parragon Book
This edition published in 2003

Parragon
Queen Street House
4 Queen Street
Bath BA1 1HE

Produced by
The Templar Company plc

Designed by Caroline Reeves

Printed and bound in China
ISBN 1-40542-032-4

Contents

Monster Chef

Troll Love

The Lost Valley

Princess Prissy and the
Stinky Bog Monster

The Fantastic Firework

The School Monster

Two Heads are Worse
Than One

The Monster No–One
Believed In

The Nasty Nice Spell

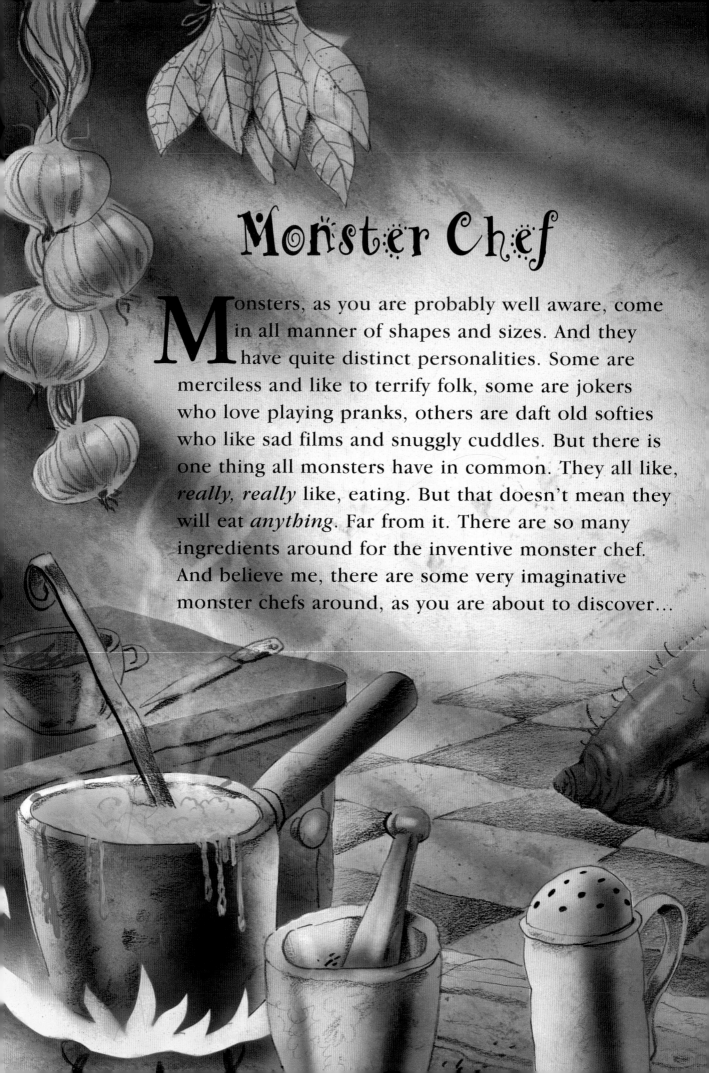

Monster Chef

Monsters, as you are probably well aware, come in all manner of shapes and sizes. And they have quite distinct personalities. Some are merciless and like to terrify folk, some are jokers who love playing pranks, others are daft old softies who like sad films and snuggly cuddles. But there is one thing all monsters have in common. They all like, *really, really* like, eating. But that doesn't mean they will eat *anything*. Far from it. There are so many ingredients around for the inventive monster chef. And believe me, there are some very imaginative monster chefs around, as you are about to discover...

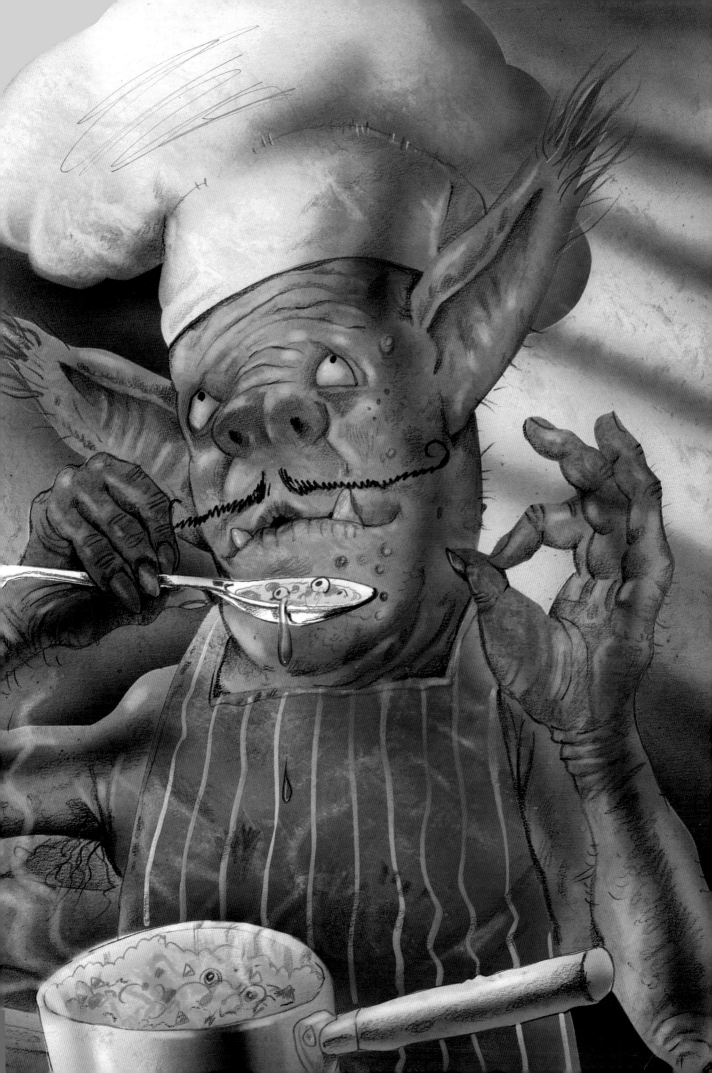

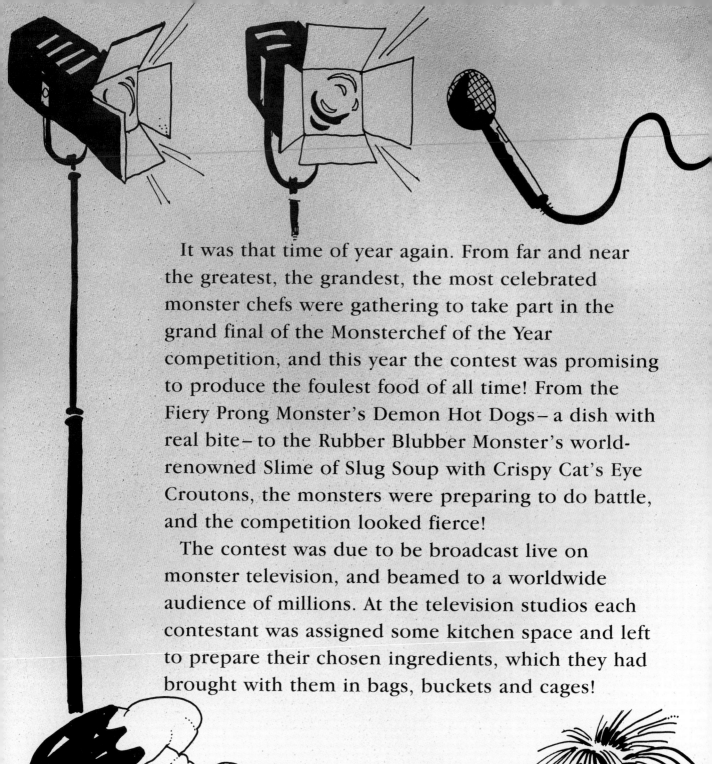

It was that time of year again. From far and near the greatest, the grandest, the most celebrated monster chefs were gathering to take part in the grand final of the Monsterchef of the Year competition, and this year the contest was promising to produce the foulest food of all time! From the Fiery Prong Monster's Demon Hot Dogs– a dish with real bite– to the Rubber Blubber Monster's world-renowned Slime of Slug Soup with Crispy Cat's Eye Croutons, the monsters were preparing to do battle, and the competition looked fierce!

The contest was due to be broadcast live on monster television, and beamed to a worldwide audience of millions. At the television studios each contestant was assigned some kitchen space and left to prepare their chosen ingredients, which they had brought with them in bags, buckets and cages!

Mr Grossmonster was hosting the show, and a panel of slavering, slobbering judges were already in place, drooling at the prospect of sampling the entries. As the studio lights dimmed, there was an excited buzz amongst the audience, and as the 'on air' sign lit up, Mr Grossmonster took the floor:

"Good evening ladies and gentlemen, and welcome to what promises to be a most exciting contest!" He went on to outline the rules and introduce the contestants. "You have one and a half hours starting from now, so good luck, and may the best monsterchef win!"

The monsters flew to their places in the kitchen, and for the next hour there was a frenzy of activity. The monsters chopped and peeled, stirred and whisked, boiled and baked. But things were not going smoothly…

Far from it. The Hairy Scary Monster threw all his arms up in horror, as a simmering pot of stagnant sludge tipped and spilt all across the stove.

"My soup base!" he cried in despair. The Bug-eyed Monster's eyes boggled as the frogs' legs in his Frog Leg and Maggot Fricassee leapt out of the pan, and bounded in all directions, causing chaos around the studio. The Stinky Gas Monster screamed as his Oven Roast Rat and Bat Blood Casserole exploded just as Mr Grossmonster passed, spattering him from head to toe. And the Rancid Fat Monster howled as his frying pan burst into flames, burning his Pig Swill Pancakes to a crisp! And that was not all. Ovens mysteriously opened, deflating Pus and Scab Soufflés and Scary Fairy Cakes. Vats of giblets and gizzards boiled over. A Sweaty Sock Stew simply got up and hopped off.

There was only one possible explanation…
It must be Gremlins!

The fact is, the other contestants had been so busy creating their own demon dishes that no-one noticed the little red container that the Foxy Trick Monster took out, and placed slyly amongst his ingredients.

It was marked 'Dangerous – Handle with Care!' And once its contents had been craftily released to wreak havoc in the kitchens, the frantic monsters were so busy dealing with their own culinary disasters, that no-one noticed what he was up to. Although they would have been rather intrigued if they had. He was making sherry trifle, which was hardly the kind of thing that had any place in a monster cooking competition. Although the other monsters would have found it

quite revolting, there was a certain type of monster that just loved it. Couldn't resist it. Couldn't get enough… Gremlins! So, once their mischievous mission was complete, the Foxy Trick Monster tempted them back to their box with generous helpings of sherry trifle, and then carried on cooking.

But time was ticking on, and the final countdown began. The distraught monsters struggled to salvage what they could from their kitchens as a frazzled Mr Grossmonster announced that their time was up. The panel of judges was called forward and the monsters presented the dismal remains of their dishes. The judges were so disgusted by the burnt offerings (not to mention disappointed at missing out on the tasting), that they disqualified each monster in turn.

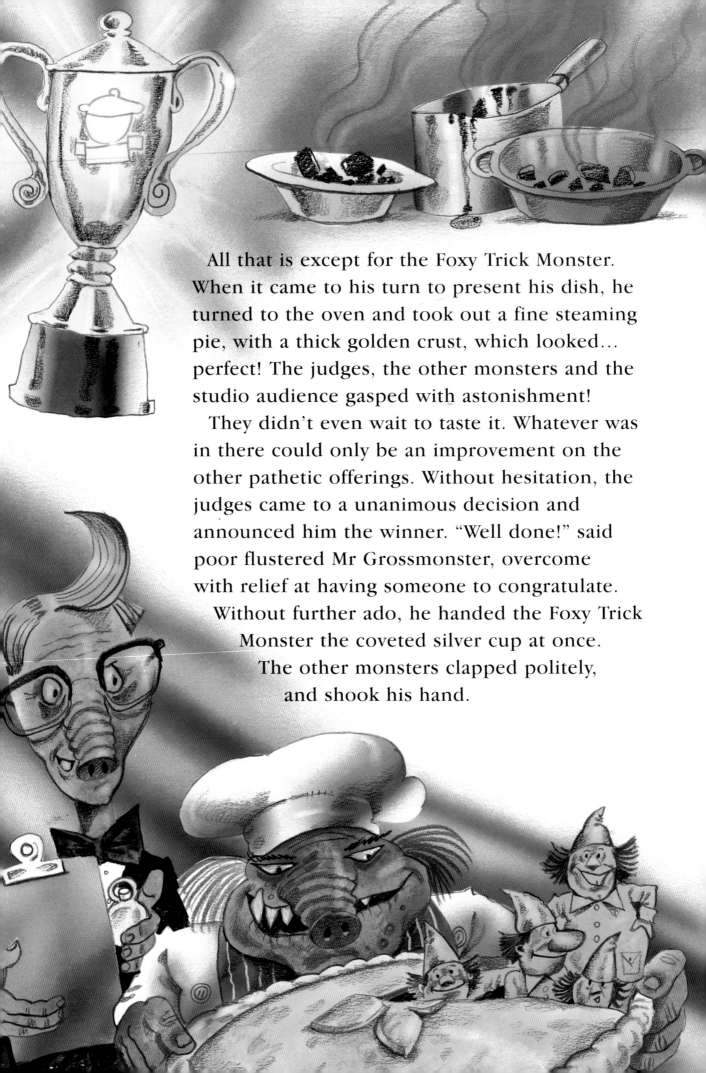

All that is except for the Foxy Trick Monster. When it came to his turn to present his dish, he turned to the oven and took out a fine steaming pie, with a thick golden crust, which looked… perfect! The judges, the other monsters and the studio audience gasped with astonishment!

They didn't even wait to taste it. Whatever was in there could only be an improvement on the other pathetic offerings. Without hesitation, the judges came to a unanimous decision and announced him the winner. "Well done!" said poor flustered Mr Grossmonster, overcome with relief at having someone to congratulate.

Without further ado, he handed the Foxy Trick Monster the coveted silver cup at once. The other monsters clapped politely, and shook his hand.

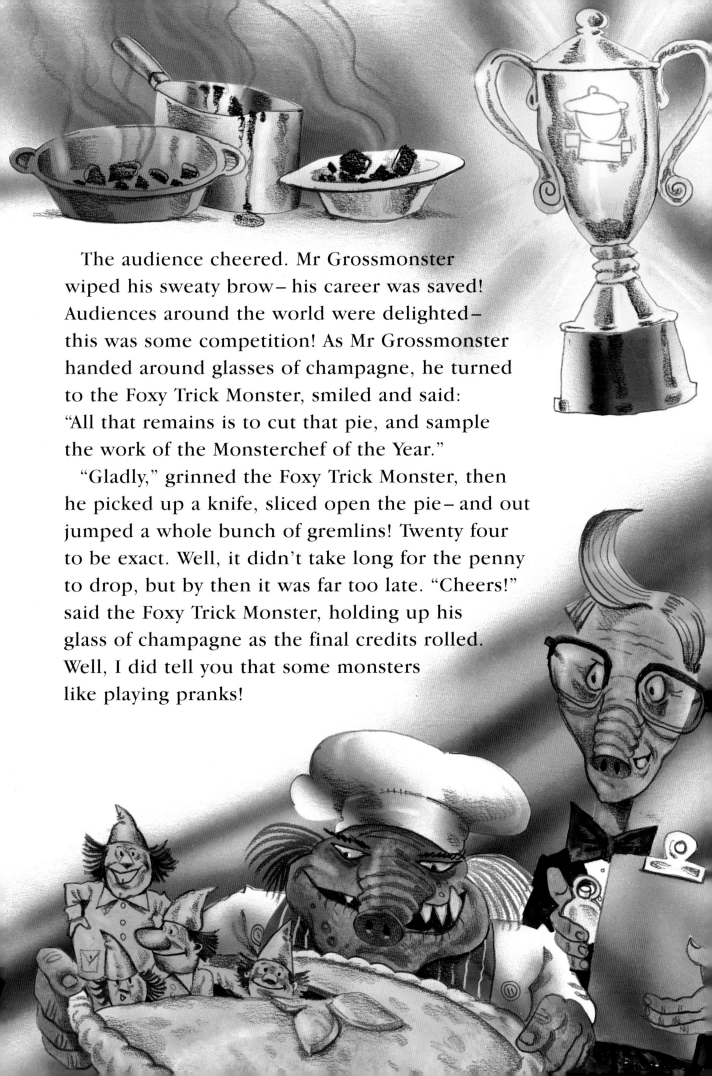

The audience cheered. Mr Grossmonster
wiped his sweaty brow– his career was saved!
Audiences around the world were delighted–
this was some competition! As Mr Grossmonster
handed around glasses of champagne, he turned
to the Foxy Trick Monster, smiled and said:
"All that remains is to cut that pie, and sample
the work of the Monsterchef of the Year."

"Gladly," grinned the Foxy Trick Monster, then
he picked up a knife, sliced open the pie– and out
jumped a whole bunch of gremlins! Twenty four
to be exact. Well, it didn't take long for the penny
to drop, but by then it was far too late. "Cheers!"
said the Foxy Trick Monster, holding up his
glass of champagne as the final credits rolled.
Well, I did tell you that some monsters
like playing pranks!

Troll Love

No-one in Fern's village had been able to go anywhere for months. They stayed in their shops and homes, or moped about on the green, waiting for something, or someone, to save them from the troll. The shepherds and the farmers kept their animals in the fields close to the centre. They didn't dare take them to the further pastures in case the troll attacked them and ate their animals.

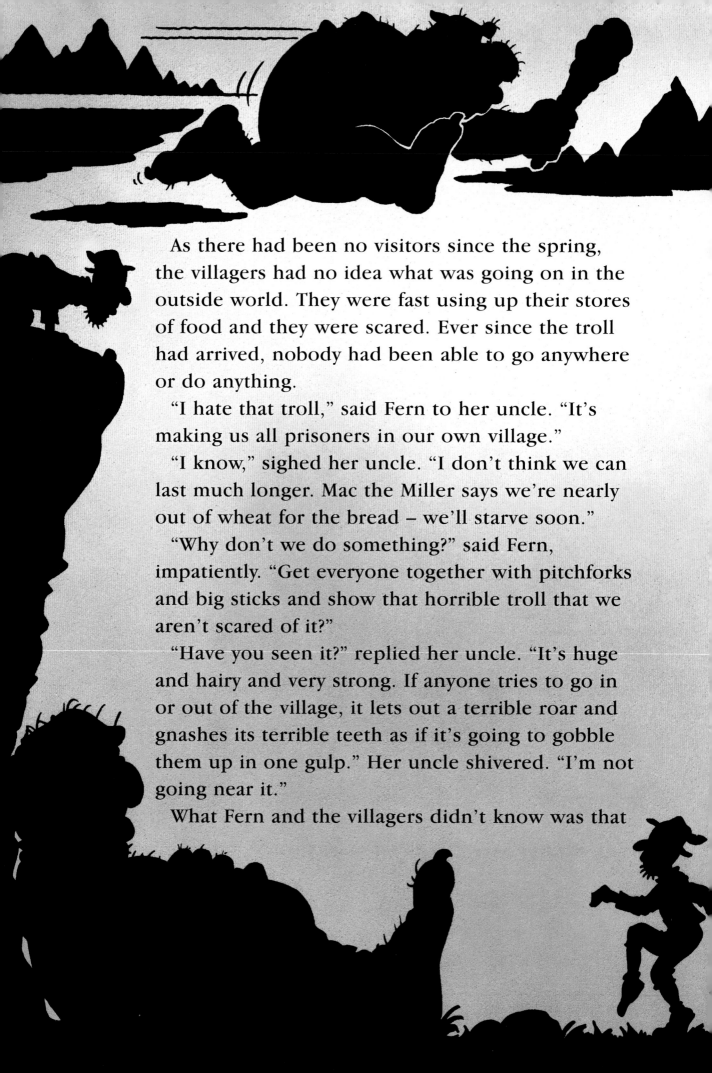

As there had been no visitors since the spring, the villagers had no idea what was going on in the outside world. They were fast using up their stores of food and they were scared. Ever since the troll had arrived, nobody had been able to go anywhere or do anything.

"I hate that troll," said Fern to her uncle. "It's making us all prisoners in our own village."

"I know," sighed her uncle. "I don't think we can last much longer. Mac the Miller says we're nearly out of wheat for the bread – we'll starve soon."

"Why don't we do something?" said Fern, impatiently. "Get everyone together with pitchforks and big sticks and show that horrible troll that we aren't scared of it?"

"Have you seen it?" replied her uncle. "It's huge and hairy and very strong. If anyone tries to go in or out of the village, it lets out a terrible roar and gnashes its terrible teeth as if it's going to gobble them up in one gulp." Her uncle shivered. "I'm not going near it."

What Fern and the villagers didn't know was that

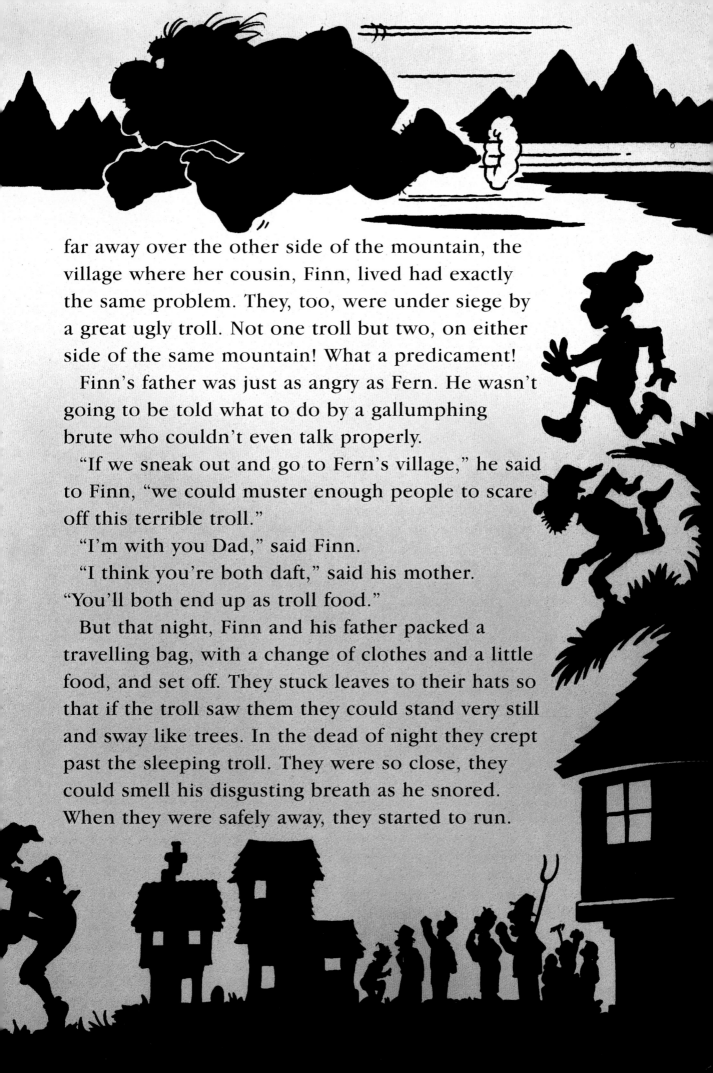

far away over the other side of the mountain, the village where her cousin, Finn, lived had exactly the same problem. They, too, were under siege by a great ugly troll. Not one troll but two, on either side of the same mountain! What a predicament!

Finn's father was just as angry as Fern. He wasn't going to be told what to do by a gallumphing brute who couldn't even talk properly.

"If we sneak out and go to Fern's village," he said to Finn, "we could muster enough people to scare off this terrible troll."

"I'm with you Dad," said Finn.

"I think you're both daft," said his mother. "You'll both end up as troll food."

But that night, Finn and his father packed a travelling bag, with a change of clothes and a little food, and set off. They stuck leaves to their hats so that if the troll saw them they could stand very still and sway like trees. In the dead of night they crept past the sleeping troll. They were so close, they could smell his disgusting breath as he snored. When they were safely away, they started to run.

"That was easy," they laughed.

They walked on over the mountain and when they were halfway down the other side they spied Fern's village below them, so small it looked like a neat little model. But, to their horror, they saw a monstrous hairy creature pacing up and down at the edge of the village, thumping his chest with his fists.

"Oh no!" said Finn in alarm. "Another troll."

They sat down. This was more than they had bargained for. There was a troll guarding their village and another guarding Fern's village. Now they were stuck between the two, with only enough food to last them a day.

"I bet our troll wouldn't think much of another one being so close," said Finn. "I bet they'd fight if they just happened to bump into each other."

"That's not a bad idea," said his father, jumping up. "Why don't we make sure they do bump into each other? And then we can stand back and watch them go for each other!"

Finn and his father, excited by this idea and not really thinking very sensibly, ran down the hill towards Fern's troll.

"Hey!" they shouted. "Big foot. Smelly breath. Over here!"

As they got closer, the troll stopped pacing and turned to face them with a grunt.

"This is it," cried Finn's father. "Run for your life!"

They turned and scrambled back up the mountain. The troll lumbered after them, making the ground shake with each massive footfall. Finn and his father stumbled down the other side, shouting and clapping their hands to make as much noise as possible. As they approached their own village, the other troll turned to see what all the noise was about. It let out a savage roar and galloped towards them. But then it saw the other troll crashing down the mountainside and stopped suddenly in its tracks. The two trolls looked at each other, then simultaneously let out a terrifying yell and tore towards each other.

Finn and his father slipped into a gap between two rocks and waited for the crash. It would be like two runaway wagons full of apples running into each other at full speed. They covered their heads and waited.

But the crash didn't come. Instead they heard the roaring subside into mellow grunts.

Finn peered out cautiously from his hiding place. The monsters were standing in front of each other and shuffling about nervously. One of them scratched its hairy tummy and kicked at a rock. The other snorted bashfully.

"What are they doing?" asked Finn.

"I don't know," whispered his father. "They just seem to be talking."

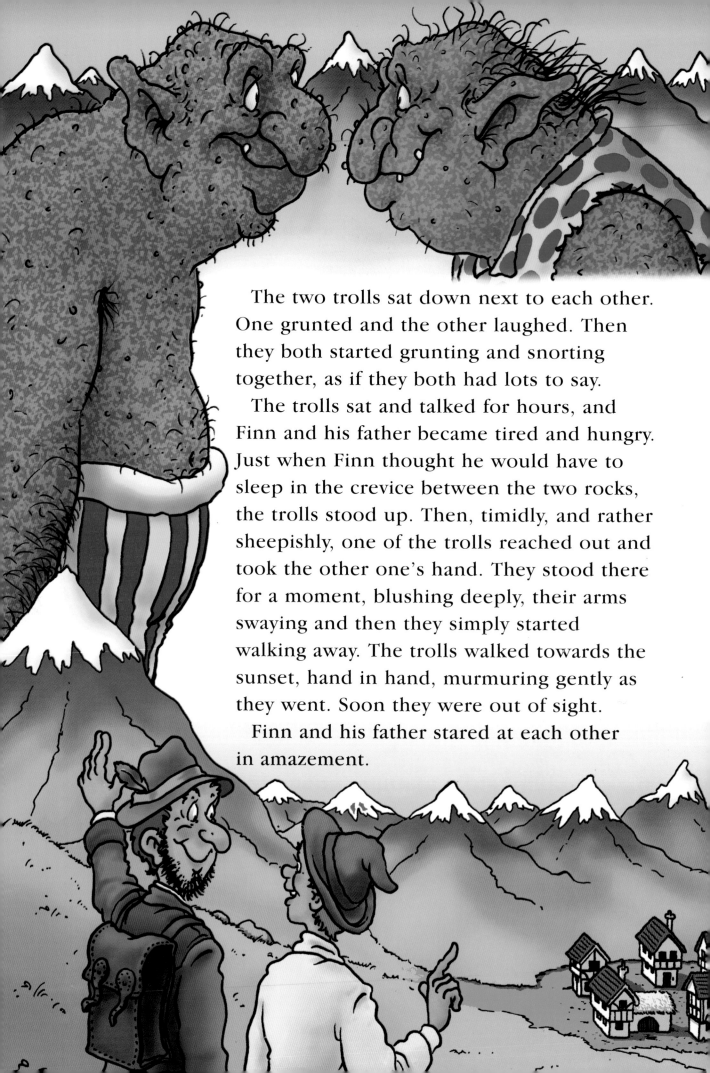

The two trolls sat down next to each other.
One grunted and the other laughed. Then
they both started grunting and snorting
together, as if they both had lots to say.

The trolls sat and talked for hours, and
Finn and his father became tired and hungry.
Just when Finn thought he would have to
sleep in the crevice between the two rocks,
the trolls stood up. Then, timidly, and rather
sheepishly, one of the trolls reached out and
took the other one's hand. They stood there
for a moment, blushing deeply, their arms
swaying and then they simply started
walking away. The trolls walked towards the
sunset, hand in hand, murmuring gently as
they went. Soon they were out of sight.

Finn and his father stared at each other
in amazement.

"If I didn't know they were cruel, foul-smelling, people-eating nasties," said Finn's father, "I'd say those two have fallen in love."

Father and son walked down to the village, arriving just as it was getting dark. There was much laughter and cheering on the village green. The villagers had seen everything and they came out to welcome the heroes.

"I think it's wonderful," said Fern's auntie. "It just goes to show you that there's s omeone for everyone and that even foul-tempered trolls can find love in this world."

But Fern had an unpleasant thought...

"Does this mean that they will live happily in the mountains and then they'll have babies," she said, gulping nervously, "and then we'll hear the thump of little hairy feet?"

Now, there's a thought to leave you with!

The Lost Valley

Deep in the hot and steamy, green jungle far away from busy cities, or even quiet little villages, there was a secret valley. Tucked away in a great gorge and watered by a mighty river that flowed over the jagged cliffs surrounding it, the valley had lain undisturbed since life on earth began.

Local people knew about it, but kept away.
Word had been passed down from as far back
as anyone knew, that a terrifying beast prowled
through its lush forests and waving grasslands.
So they called it the Valley of the Great Devils
and warned everyone stay away.

They were wise to be afraid. Something very
dreadful did lurk in that valley – the last living
Gigantosaurus in the world.

Alas, not everyone was as sensible as the people
living nearest to the Valley. A nasty circus owner
called Terrible Tony had heard about it by chance,
while tracking down the most magnificent wild
animals he could find to catch for his travelling
circus. What Tony enjoyed most was capturing
the fiercest animals he could find, and then
teaching them tricks to make them look stupid.

As soon as he heard of a hidden valley with a
dreadful secret, he was determined to find it.

'With any luck,' he thought, his eyes glinting wickedly, 'it will be some kind of dangerous animal and I can catch it and turn it into a big, stupid pussy cat!'

Tony decided to mount a hunting expedition immediately. He advertised for a guide and a cook to go with him but no-one would– they were all too frightened. That should have put him off but it only made him more eager to go.

"Terrible Tony is scared of nothing," he told anyone who tried to dissuade him.

Not knowing what he would be up against, he armed himself with stun guns, giant nets and even a lassoo. He stocked up with provisions, made a sketch map and loaded everything into an inflatable raft. Then he set sail, all alone.

It took Tony a week to reach the valley, paddling down the river that flowed into it. The current was with him and so he made good progress.

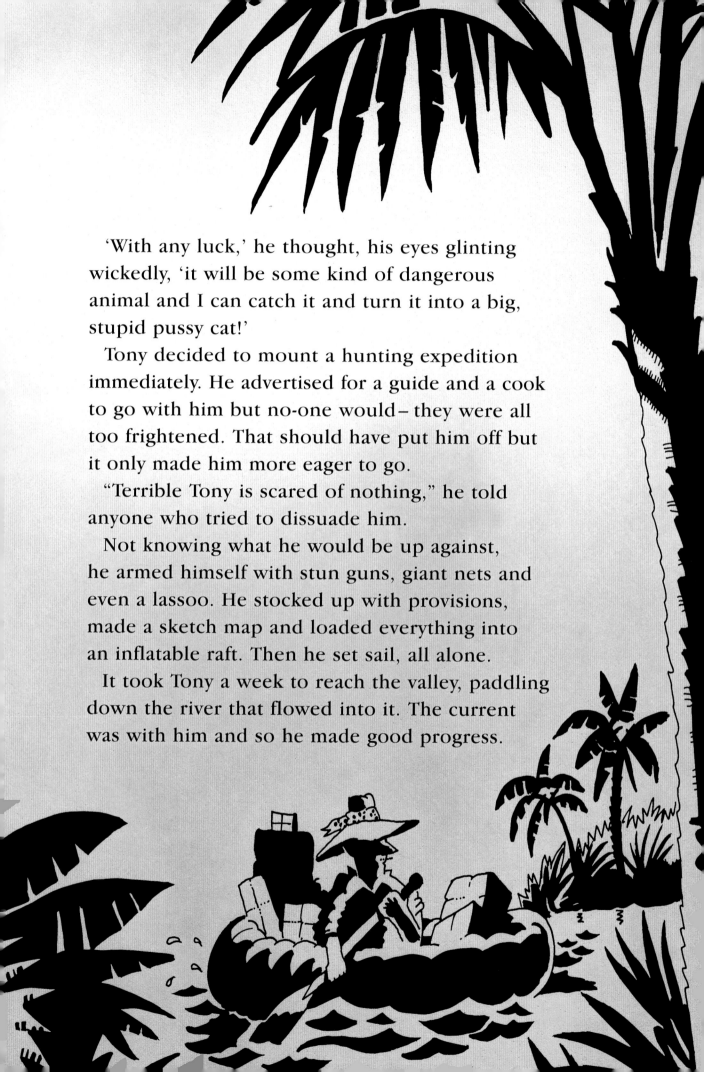

The further he travelled into the jungle, the wilder it became. Often, he couldn't see the sky at all through the thick canopy of leaves overhead. The air was full of noises. Parrots squawked and monkeys chattered in the trees around him. Elephants trumpeted from the banks and crocodiles snapped at him.

Then, one morning, Tony heard a very different sound – a bloodcurdling roar. All the animal noises stopped and there was an eerie silence.

"Pipe down, pussycat," Tony shouted, paddling even faster.

No-one else had ventured into the valley, they had just looked down from the top of the mountainous gorge on either side. Tony had been told that the river flowed through it but he had no idea that it crashed down over huge boulders.

Descending into the valley was like doing the scariest water ride imaginable again and again.

One moment he was paddling along, and the next he was nose-diving over the edge of sheer rock. The last waterfall was the worst of all. It was so steep that the raft took off. As Tony clung on desperately, he sailed over the tree tops before coming to land in one of the shallow pits that criss-crossed a lush plain. There was something odd about the shape and pattern of those pits, then Tony realised what they were – giant footprints!

Even though each print was wide and deep enough to hold his entire raft, he was still sure that whatever the creature was, it would be no match for him. Foolish Tony *still* wasn't worried!

The earth began to shudder – something was coming that was so enormous, it was making the ground shake.

The trees parted and a giant lizard burst out of the jungle. It was as long as a town square and as tall as a skyscraper. It was the rarest creature in the world, the last of a long line of Gigantosauri that had lived in the valley since every other dinosaur had become extinct.

If Tony had had any sense, he would have run for his life.

Instead he yelled. "Over here stupid!"

The Gigantosaurus couldn't hear him. Tony's shouts sounded like tiny, far away squeaks. However, it had spotted the bright orange raft and made straight for it.

The enormous creature stopped just before it reached the raft and sniffed the air. Then it opened its huge jaws and gave a terrific, earsplitting roar.

"You don't scare me, you big, overgrown alligator!" shouted Tony, guessing the monster had scented him. The Gigantosaurus threw back its head and bellowed so loudly that the sound echoed through the jungle like thunder and the villagers shook in their shoes. Tony fired a round of darts from his stun gun at the huge reptile and waited for it to keel over unconscious, so that he could tie it up.

But instead the Gigantosaurus just shook itself lazily as all the tranquillised darts fell harmlessly to the ground. It studied the tiny red-faced creature which was making such a horrible noise, when it should have fallen silent in the presence of the King of the Valley. Then it took action to remove it.

Swiftly, it bent down and seized Tony in its mighty jaws. But the Gigantosaurus didn't

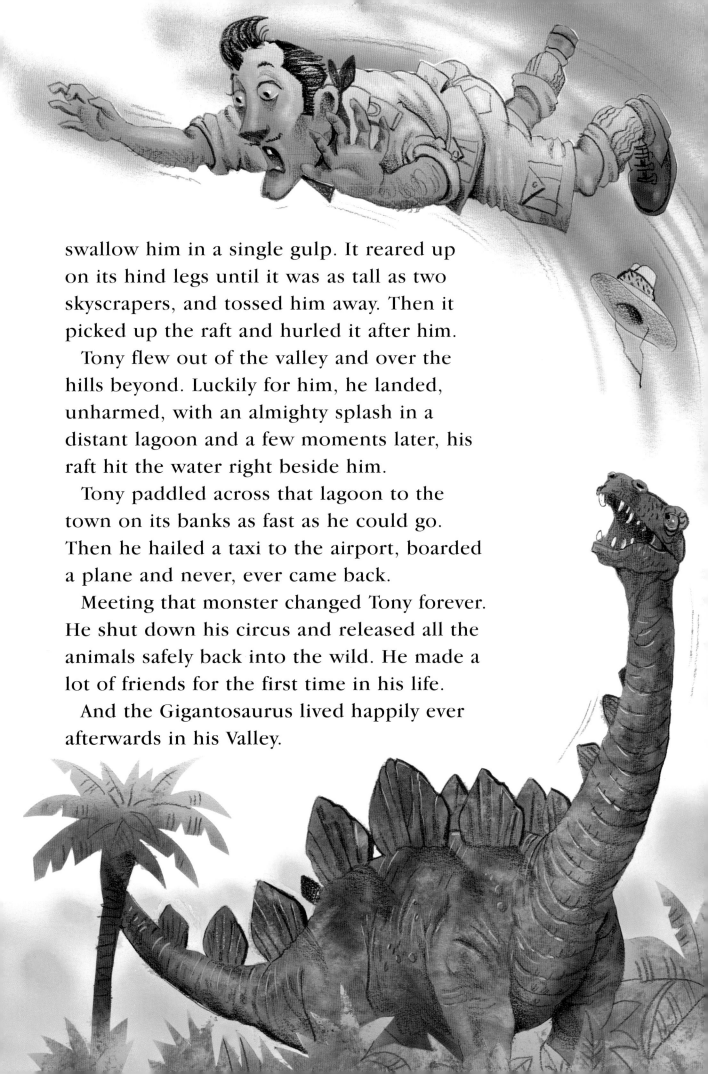

swallow him in a single gulp. It reared up on its hind legs until it was as tall as two skyscrapers, and tossed him away. Then it picked up the raft and hurled it after him.

Tony flew out of the valley and over the hills beyond. Luckily for him, he landed, unharmed, with an almighty splash in a distant lagoon and a few moments later, his raft hit the water right beside him.

Tony paddled across that lagoon to the town on its banks as fast as he could go. Then he hailed a taxi to the airport, boarded a plane and never, ever came back.

Meeting that monster changed Tony forever. He shut down his circus and released all the animals safely back into the wild. He made a lot of friends for the first time in his life.

And the Gigantosaurus lived happily ever afterwards in his Valley.

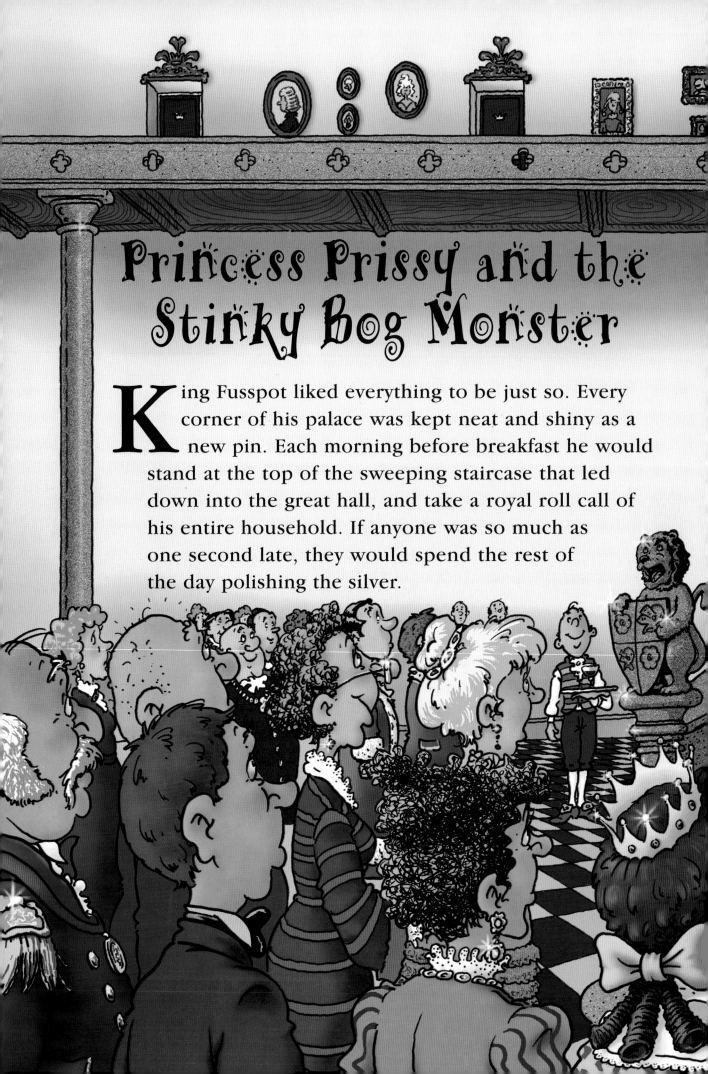

Princess Prissy and the Stinky Bog Monster

K ing Fusspot liked everything to be just so. Every corner of his palace was kept neat and shiny as a new pin. Each morning before breakfast he would stand at the top of the sweeping staircase that led down into the great hall, and take a royal roll call of his entire household. If anyone was so much as one second late, they would spend the rest of the day polishing the silver.

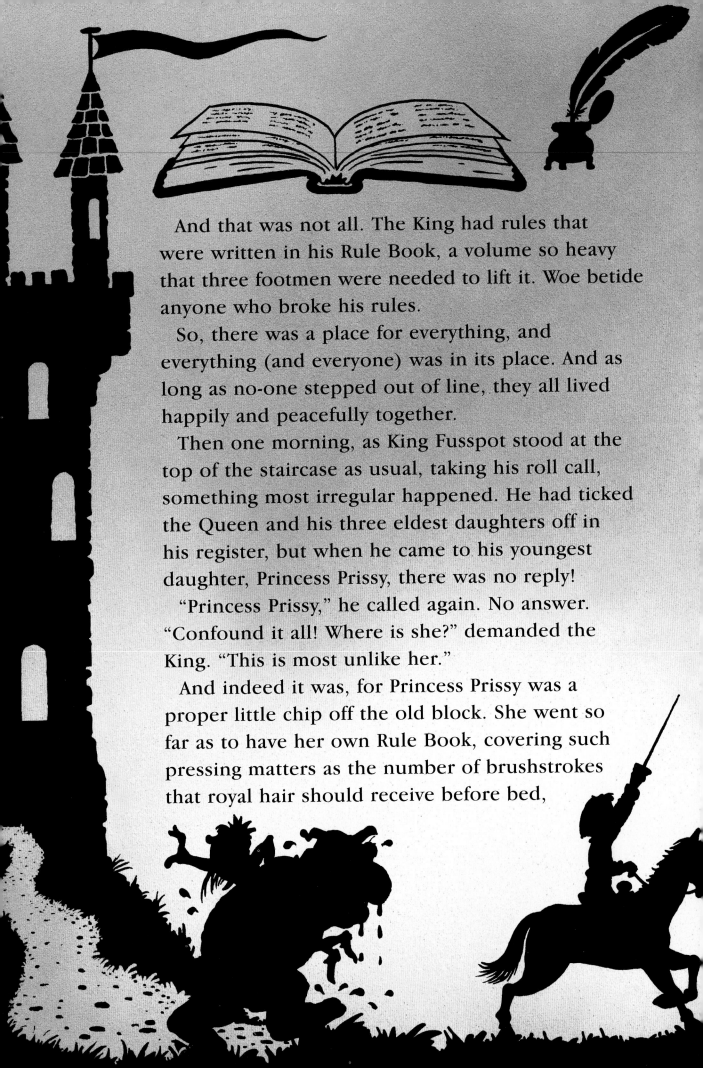

And that was not all. The King had rules that were written in his Rule Book, a volume so heavy that three footmen were needed to lift it. Woe betide anyone who broke his rules.

So, there was a place for everything, and everything (and everyone) was in its place. And as long as no-one stepped out of line, they all lived happily and peacefully together.

Then one morning, as King Fusspot stood at the top of the staircase as usual, taking his roll call, something most irregular happened. He had ticked the Queen and his three eldest daughters off in his register, but when he came to his youngest daughter, Princess Prissy, there was no reply!

"Princess Prissy," he called again. No answer. "Confound it all! Where is she?" demanded the King. "This is most unlike her."

And indeed it was, for Princess Prissy was a proper little chip off the old block. She went so far as to have her own Rule Book, covering such pressing matters as the number of brushstrokes that royal hair should receive before bed,

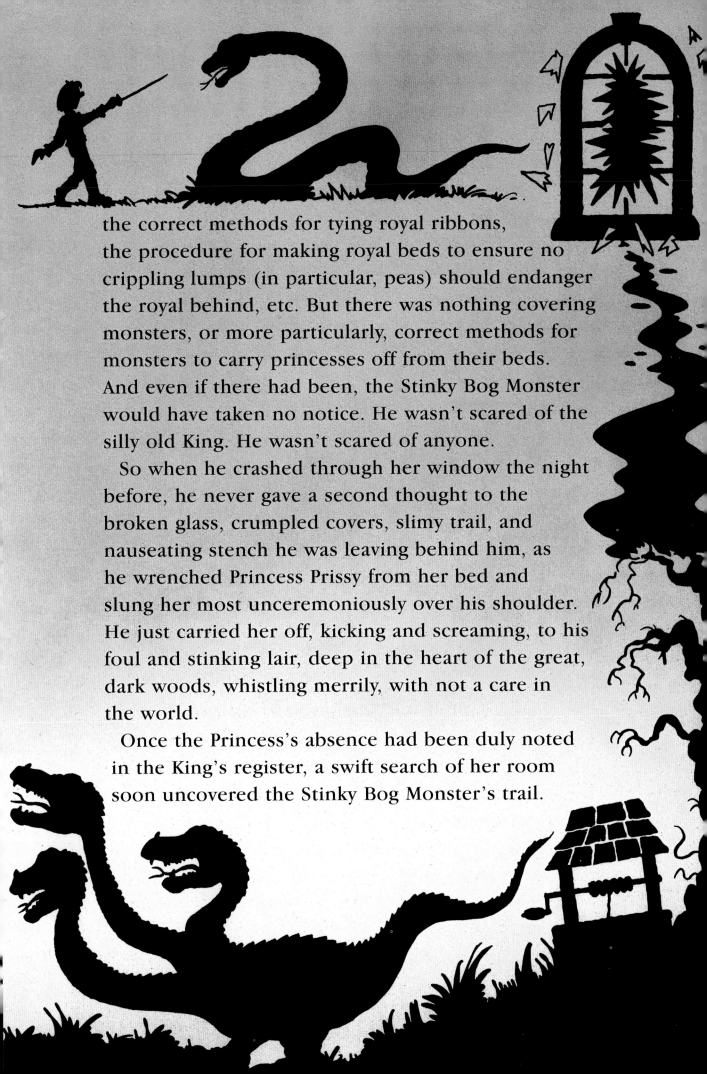

the correct methods for tying royal ribbons,
the procedure for making royal beds to ensure no
crippling lumps (in particular, peas) should endanger
the royal behind, etc. But there was nothing covering
monsters, or more particularly, correct methods for
monsters to carry princesses off from their beds.
And even if there had been, the Stinky Bog Monster
would have taken no notice. He wasn't scared of the
silly old King. He wasn't scared of anyone.

So when he crashed through her window the night
before, he never gave a second thought to the
broken glass, crumpled covers, slimy trail, and
nauseating stench he was leaving behind him, as
he wrenched Princess Prissy from her bed and
slung her most unceremoniously over his shoulder.
He just carried her off, kicking and screaming, to his
foul and stinking lair, deep in the heart of the great,
dark woods, whistling merrily, with not a care in
the world.

Once the Princess's absence had been duly noted
in the King's register, a swift search of her room
soon uncovered the Stinky Bog Monster's trail.

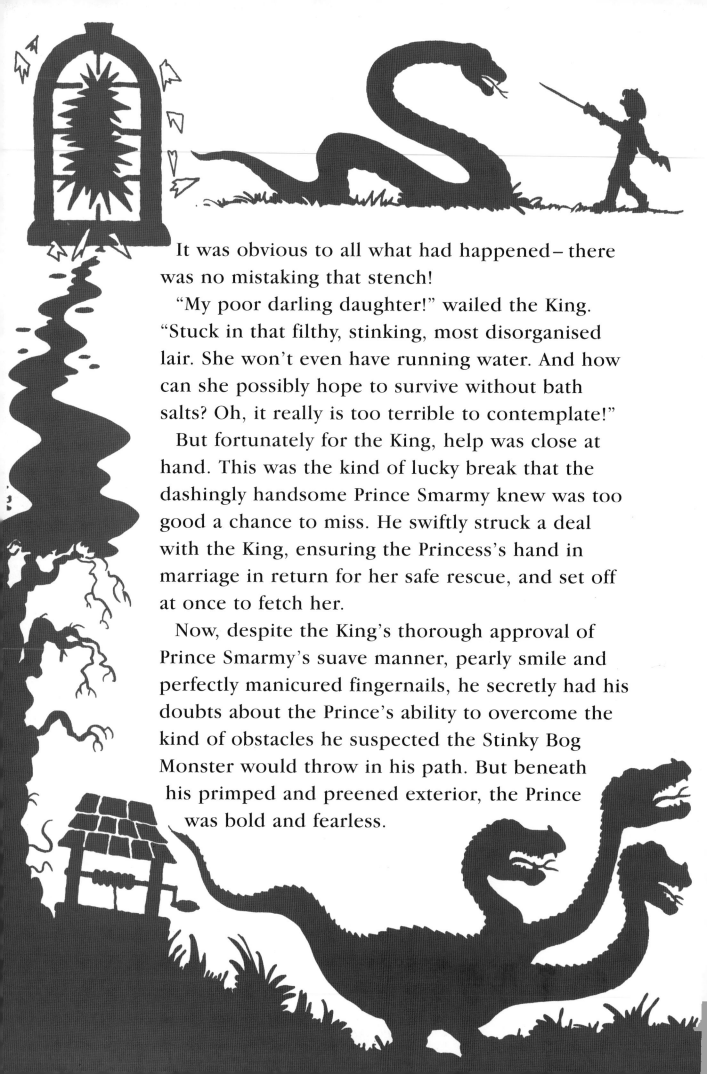

It was obvious to all what had happened – there was no mistaking that stench!

"My poor darling daughter!" wailed the King. "Stuck in that filthy, stinking, most disorganised lair. She won't even have running water. And how can she possibly hope to survive without bath salts? Oh, it really is too terrible to contemplate!"

But fortunately for the King, help was close at hand. This was the kind of lucky break that the dashingly handsome Prince Smarmy knew was too good a chance to miss. He swiftly struck a deal with the King, ensuring the Princess's hand in marriage in return for her safe rescue, and set off at once to fetch her.

Now, despite the King's thorough approval of Prince Smarmy's suave manner, pearly smile and perfectly manicured fingernails, he secretly had his doubts about the Prince's ability to overcome the kind of obstacles he suspected the Stinky Bog Monster would throw in his path. But beneath his primped and preened exterior, the Prince was bold and fearless.

What is more, he was absolutely crackers about Princess Prissy, so he was not about to let anything stand in his way.

Deep in the heart of the great, dark woods, Prince Smarmy had to battle his way past demons and dragons, vampires and vipers, ogres and trolls to reach the Stinky Bog Monster's lair.

"No problem," smirked the Prince smugly, brushing himself down after a rather unpleasant encounter with a three-headed beast. And before long, he arrived at the entrance to the Stinky Bog Monster's loathsome lair itself! Now all he had to do was retrieve the Princess, whisk her back to the palace, and he'd be home, safe and up the aisle in no time.

However, Prince Smarmy, unlike the Stinky Bog Monster, was quite familiar with the Princess's Rule Book (not to mention the King's) and knew all the proper procedures to follow

when rescuing princesses. Most important of all, he knew he should appear on a gleaming white charger. While he was hiding behind a tree cleaning all the mud, gunge and bits of old troll off his horse, he caught sight of her...

She was leaning over a well, just outside the entrance to the Stinky Bog Monster's lair, pulling up a bucket of reeking, green, stagnant water. Her clothes were torn and covered in stains, her hair was a filthy, matted mess, crawling with bugs, her face was smeared with mud and grime, and her eyes gleamed and glinted wildly. But despite all this, there was no mistaking her. It really was Princess Prissy! The Prince's heart was torn with anguish. His darling Princess – what had that beastly Bog Monster done to her? Just then, as the Prince prepared to leap onto his charger to rescue her, the Stinky Bog Monster himself appeared.

Princess Prissy turned and greeted him with a blackened, gappy smile.

"Hello there, Boggy darling! Come and smell how nice and stagnant the water is today! Our tea should taste really disgusting with this!" And with that, she reached out, took his hand and planted a slobbery kiss on his cheek! As the Prince cried out in horror, the Princess and her Bog Monster turned and caught sight of him.

"Oh, yuk, not you!" spat the Princess. "If you've come to rescue me, you can get lost, I'm not coming home – ever!"

"Don't be ridiculous Prissy," cried the horrified Prince. "You can't stay here. Look at yourself – you're hideous! He's got you hypnotised. But don't worry, you'll soon come to your senses..."

"Oh, but I have come to my senses," hissed Princess Prissy. "At last I've escaped all those silly rules. All that niceness, and prettiness, and good manners. I'm free! I like being rude and horrible

and hideous, it's really rather fun. I've got my darling Stinky Bog Monster to thank for it, and you're too late– we got married last night!" Then Princess Prissy and the Bog Monster let out cackling laughs and staggered back inside.

There was nothing else for it. Prince Smarmy had to admit defeat, turn on his heels, and head home. He wondered what the King would say. It would certainly mess up his neat register. Then he noticed a deep, muddy puddle in front of him.

'Why not?' he thought, and rode his clean, white horse straight through it, splattering both of them with black, sticky mud. Then he saw another one. This time he made his horse jump into it. He laughed out loud.

'You never know,' he thought. 'Perhaps the Princess was right, after all. Perhaps some rules are just too silly.'

And he rode through every single puddle until he got back to the castle.

The Fantastic Firework

Whoosh! A fountain of gold stars fell twinkling to earth through the night sky. It was Bonfire Night in the village of Upper Redding and a big crowd had gathered to enjoy the spectacular fireworks display.

High above them, someone else was watching, too.

"Ah! Home again!" said Ag the Alien, as he zoomed overhead in his brand new supercharged spaceship before he came in to land.

But Ag wasn't anywhere near his home. His planet was light years away across the galaxy. He was horribly lost and, worse still, he had no idea.

Without realising it, Ag had activated the hyper thrust device that was a special feature of his super deluxe spacecraft. And the instant Ag had touched that small silver button, he had shot halfway across the universe. By an extraordinary coincidence, it just so happened that Ag's family, far, far away, was also having a fireworks display that very same night.

'I must be late!' Ag thought anxiously, as he set the co-ordinates to land. 'They've already started!'

Meanwhile, down below, a boy called Mike tugged at his father's arm.

"Hey! Look over there, Dad," he cried. "That's a really strange-looking rocket. It's coming down, not going up!"

But his father wasn't paying any attention to him and no-one else seemed to have noticed the silver streak shooting down through the sky. The mysterious firework was falling some way away from the main display. It was heading for a clump of trees on the other side of the bonfire.

'I wonder what on earth it is,' Mike thought. And he set off to investigate on his own.

The strange rocket wasn't earthly at all, of course. It was Ag's spacecraft.

Still blissfully unaware that he was light years away from home, the alien had made a perfect landing and was feeling rather pleased with himself. Until he looked through his skyscreen, that is, and then he had a dreadful shock.

"This isn't my party!" Ag gasped. "Where's my house? Where's my garden?"

It was a very nasty surprise.

Ag hastily pressed the 'Where Am I?' switch, and a message flashed at the top of the instrument panel.

It read: 'You are on Planet Earth...Have a nice day.'

"Earth!" shrieked Ag. "But that's on the other side of the galaxy!"

He realised then that he must have activated the hyper thrust and that he'd better press it again to get back, when something happened that stopped him in his tracks.

At that moment, a couple of aerial fountains blossomed across the sky in a brilliant flash of blue and yellow. Now, Ag loved fireworks. In fact, everyone did on his planet. He was always on the lookout for exciting new ones, and the sight of the Upper Redding fireworks display had just given him a very good idea.

'Just think how thrilled everyone at home would be,' Ag thought, 'if I let off some fireworks that they had never ever seen before. I'd better just pop out and get some.'

So he armed himself with a laser gun, just in case it was not a friendly planet, jumped out of the spacecraft and hurried off in the direction of the Upper Redding bonfire.

Unfortunately, it was at exactly that moment that Mike arrived, hot on the trail of the strange rocket.

Bang! They ran straight into each other.

"Aagh!" yelled Mike at the sight of the alien.

"Do we know each other?" asked Ag, feeling very confused. "Pleased to meet you."

He had been about to blow the odd-looking creature to smithereens with his laser megablaster. But it seemed to recognise him. It had certainly said his name very enthusiastically.

Mike was also feeling very confused. But he saw the laser megablaster and quickly decided it would be wiser to make friends, as that was what the alien seemed to want to do.

"Er, pleased to meet you, too," he replied.

So they shook hands, or rather Ag shook a hand and Mike shook a tentacle. It felt very odd and rather squashy for both of them.

Mike was longing to ask Ag lots of questions, like where he came from and what he was doing. But the alien was in too much of a hurry.

"Now," said Ag. "You must take me to your display. I need your fireworks immediately for a party back home tonight."

Mike gulped. He couldn't think why an alien would want fireworks and he was terrified of what might happen if Ag appeared at the bonfire. The sight of him would be enough to send everyone running in every direction. Even worse, the alien might be tempted to use his laser megablaster on them. He had to think of some way of ensuring that Ag got his fireworks but somehow wasn't spotted.

"I'll get them for you," Mike replied hastily, wondering how he was going to remove any fireworks without anyone noticing, but realising he had no choice. "You can stay here."

Mike ran off. He was relieved to see that Ag had settled down to wait for his return, but what could he bring back? It would have to be something really good to satisfy the alien.

As he got nearer the bonfire, Mike got even more worried. But then he caught sight of something large, standing by itself, some way away from crowd and he realised he'd found the very thing. It was the grand finale to the display, a giant illuminated display that lit up in the shape of the village name, made out of multi-coloured catherine wheels. That would cause a sensation on an alien planet – but it was too heavy for him to lift!

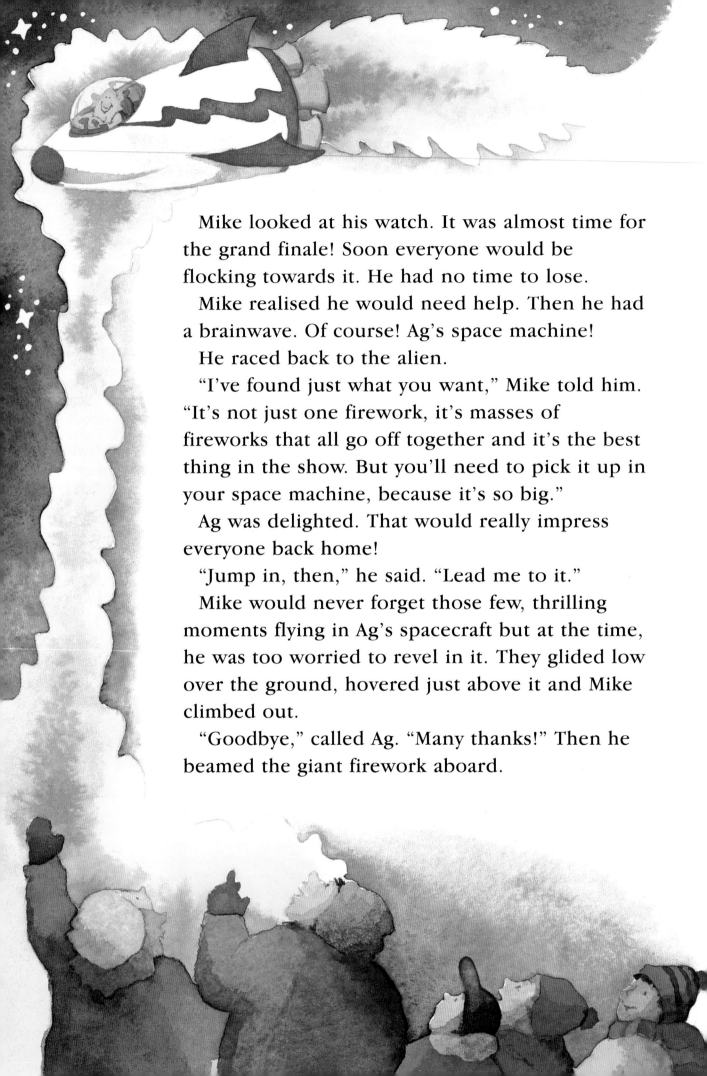

Mike looked at his watch. It was almost time for the grand finale! Soon everyone would be flocking towards it. He had no time to lose.

Mike realised he would need help. Then he had a brainwave. Of course! Ag's space machine!

He raced back to the alien.

"I've found just what you want," Mike told him. "It's not just one firework, it's masses of fireworks that all go off together and it's the best thing in the show. But you'll need to pick it up in your space machine, because it's so big."

Ag was delighted. That would really impress everyone back home!

"Jump in, then," he said. "Lead me to it."

Mike would never forget those few, thrilling moments flying in Ag's spacecraft but at the time, he was too worried to revel in it. They glided low over the ground, hovered just above it and Mike climbed out.

"Goodbye," called Ag. "Many thanks!" Then he beamed the giant firework aboard.

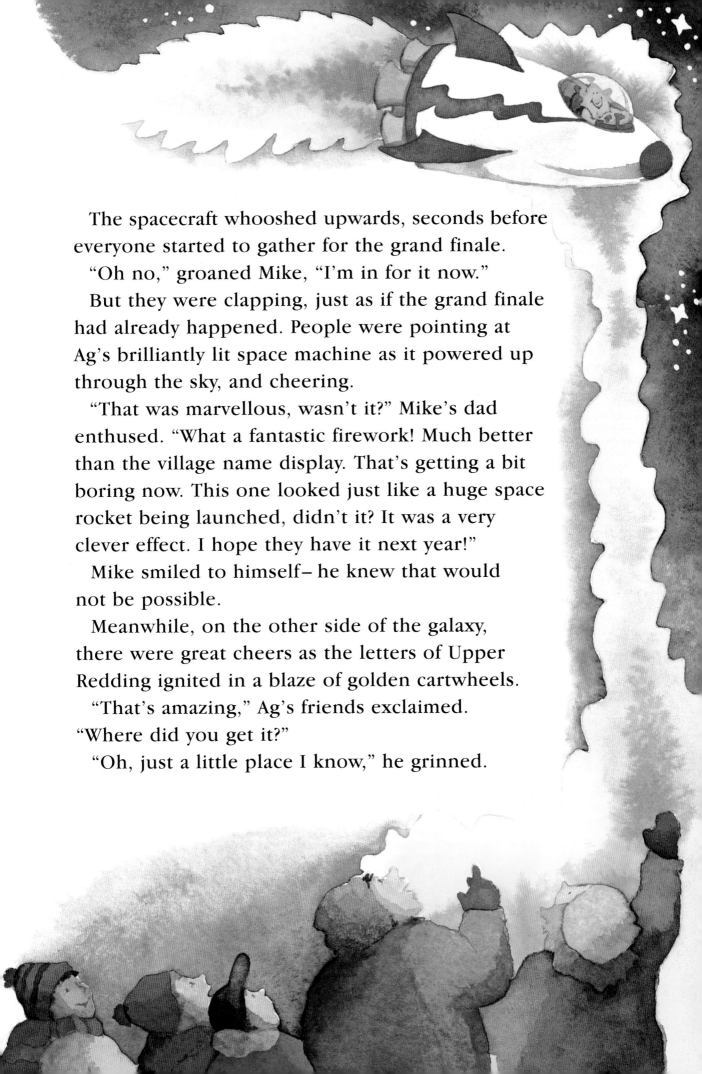

The spacecraft whooshed upwards, seconds before everyone started to gather for the grand finale.

"Oh no," groaned Mike, "I'm in for it now."

But they were clapping, just as if the grand finale had already happened. People were pointing at Ag's brilliantly lit space machine as it powered up through the sky, and cheering.

"That was marvellous, wasn't it?" Mike's dad enthused. "What a fantastic firework! Much better than the village name display. That's getting a bit boring now. This one looked just like a huge space rocket being launched, didn't it? It was a very clever effect. I hope they have it next year!"

Mike smiled to himself– he knew that would not be possible.

Meanwhile, on the other side of the galaxy, there were great cheers as the letters of Upper Redding ignited in a blaze of golden cartwheels.

"That's amazing," Ag's friends exclaimed. "Where did you get it?"

"Oh, just a little place I know," he grinned.

The School Monster

Some schools have a cat, a fluffy rabbit or a pair of fish. St Stephen's School was very different – it had a pet monster. Mortimer Monster, as he was known, was as big as the bike shed but luckily he didn't live in it. In the winter he liked to wrap himself around the boiler house because it was lovely and warm. In the summer he sunned himself by the pool and let the schoolchildren use his tail as a waterslide.

Mortimer helped out in other ways, too. He was particularly useful during games, when he could shoot out one of his many long, hairy arms to catch balls before they disappeared into the bushes. No-one liked searching for them there because they were full of thorns and nettles and they always came out covered in scratches and stings.

It was because someone searched for a lost ball in the bushes that Mortimer was at St Stephen's School at all.

It was little Jimmy Roberts from class 4A who had found Mortimer, but he thought he'd just found an unusual football.

Jimmy had to stay on after games to look for the ball he'd kicked into the bushes instead of in the goal. He'd been told he couldn't go home until he'd found the ball. Jimmy was feeling cross with everyone and very sorry for himself.

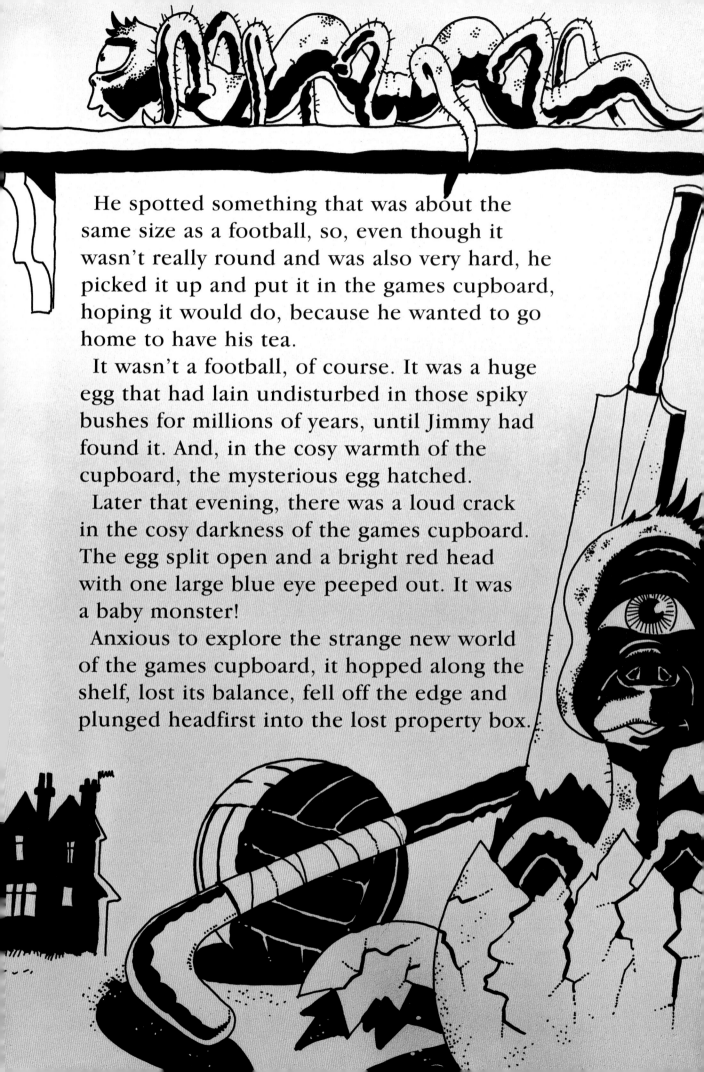

He spotted something that was about the same size as a football, so, even though it wasn't really round and was also very hard, he picked it up and put it in the games cupboard, hoping it would do, because he wanted to go home to have his tea.

It wasn't a football, of course. It was a huge egg that had lain undisturbed in those spiky bushes for millions of years, until Jimmy had found it. And, in the cosy warmth of the cupboard, the mysterious egg hatched.

Later that evening, there was a loud crack in the cosy darkness of the games cupboard. The egg split open and a bright red head with one large blue eye peeped out. It was a baby monster!

Anxious to explore the strange new world of the games cupboard, it hopped along the shelf, lost its balance, fell off the edge and plunged headfirst into the lost property box.

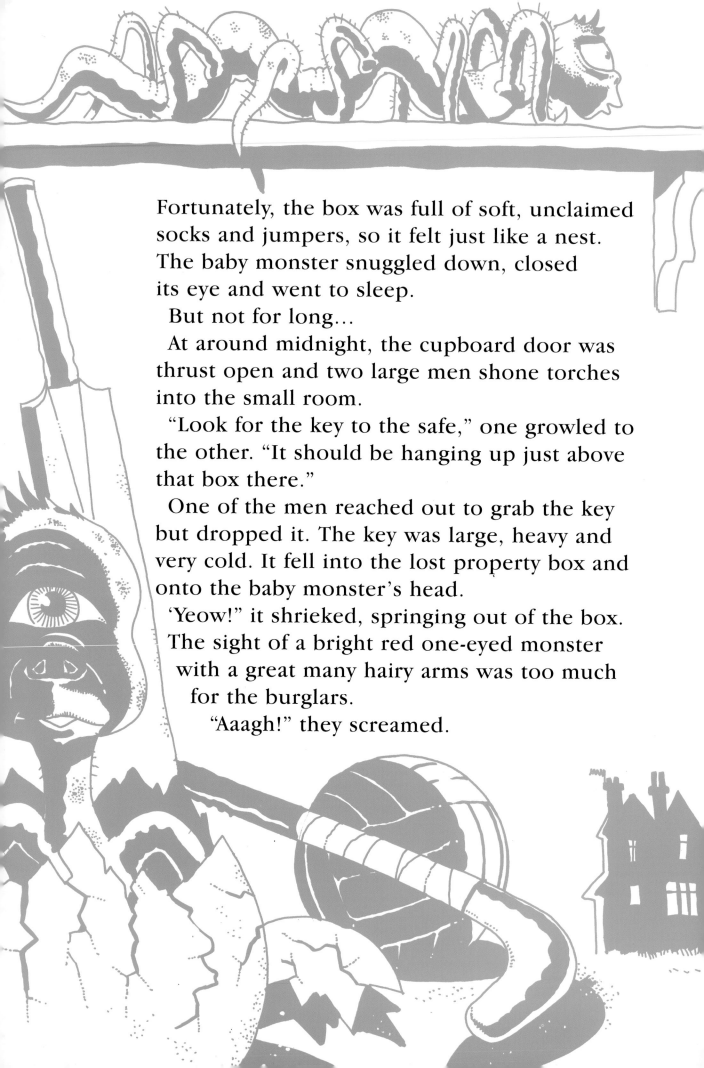

Fortunately, the box was full of soft, unclaimed socks and jumpers, so it felt just like a nest. The baby monster snuggled down, closed its eye and went to sleep.

But not for long…

At around midnight, the cupboard door was thrust open and two large men shone torches into the small room.

"Look for the key to the safe," one growled to the other. "It should be hanging up just above that box there."

One of the men reached out to grab the key but dropped it. The key was large, heavy and very cold. It fell into the lost property box and onto the baby monster's head.

'Yeow!" it shrieked, springing out of the box. The sight of a bright red one-eyed monster with a great many hairy arms was too much for the burglars.

"Aaagh!" they screamed.

The men shot backwards out of the door and tripped over each other in their panic.

"Get off me!" they yelled, each thinking they were being attacked by the monster. In their panic, they hit out wildly with their torches, knocked each other unconscious and fell heavily to the floor.

Alerted by the noise, Mr Maguire the school caretaker raced to the scene. He guessed intruders had got in and he feared that they would have escaped with their booty. He could hardly believe his eyes when he saw two large men lying unconscious on the floor outside the games cupboard. School trophies they were trying to steal were scattered on the floor.

"Caught in the act!" he gasped. "But I don't know how!"

Then Mr Maguire saw the monster. However, unlike the burglars, he didn't scream and try to run. Instead, he said, rather surprisingly, "Well look at you! How sweet!"

And he was quite right. The baby monster did look very sweet. It was back in the lost property box again, tucked up in a school jumper and it looked up at Mr Maguire with such a sad blue eye that it melted his heart. He picked it up very carefully and when it didn't try and bite him but just gurgled in a harmless, babylike way, he tickled it under the chin.

The monster squeaked with pleasure and waved his bright red arms about. At that moment, the burglars regained consciousness.

'Help!' thought Mr Maguire. 'They're going to kill me!'

But he needn't have worried. The two large men took one look at the baby monster, screamed in terror and ran for their lives.

That's when Mr Maguire had an extremely good idea.

"You would make a wonderful security guard," he told the monster. "I'll make you a nice home here and you can stop St Stephen's from being burgled again."

And that's exactly what happened. Mr Maguire told Miss Brown, the head teacher, all about the burglars and she agreed it would be very useful to have a monster to guard the school. Then, Miss Brown called a special assembly and introduced the baby monster to everyone. Like Mr Maguire and Miss Brown – but not

like the burglars, of course – they saw what a friendly little creature it was and they all wanted him to stay. After much debate, they named him Mortimer.

At first they were anxious that Mortimer wouldn't be scary enough to frighten intruders away, but they soon changed their minds when he started to grow. After one month of school food, Mortimer was too big for the games cupboard and by the next month, he was too big to get through the front door of the school. Luckily, he stopped growing then!

Everyone agreed that St Stephen's monster was the best thing that had ever happened. No-one ever guessed how Mortimer came to be there, not even little Jimmy Roberts – and he found him!

Two Heads Are Worse Than One

Clay and Rye were fed up. They were fed up with their bossy parents, always giving them jobs to do. It was 'bring those turnips in,' and 'have you fed the chickens?' from dawn till dusk. So, one evening, Clay and Rye decided to run away. As darkness crept in, they crept out, away from the village and across the fields.

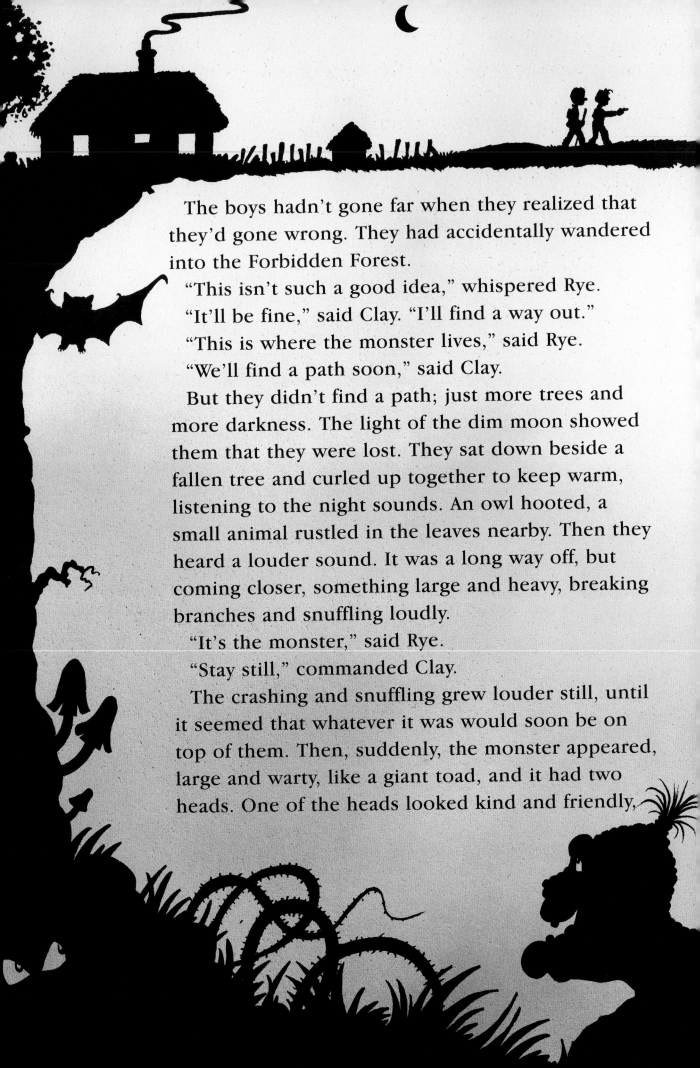

The boys hadn't gone far when they realized that they'd gone wrong. They had accidentally wandered into the Forbidden Forest.

"This isn't such a good idea," whispered Rye.

"It'll be fine," said Clay. "I'll find a way out."

"This is where the monster lives," said Rye.

"We'll find a path soon," said Clay.

But they didn't find a path; just more trees and more darkness. The light of the dim moon showed them that they were lost. They sat down beside a fallen tree and curled up together to keep warm, listening to the night sounds. An owl hooted, a small animal rustled in the leaves nearby. Then they heard a louder sound. It was a long way off, but coming closer, something large and heavy, breaking branches and snuffling loudly.

"It's the monster," said Rye.

"Stay still," commanded Clay.

The crashing and snuffling grew louder still, until it seemed that whatever it was would soon be on top of them. Then, suddenly, the monster appeared, large and warty, like a giant toad, and it had two heads. One of the heads looked kind and friendly,

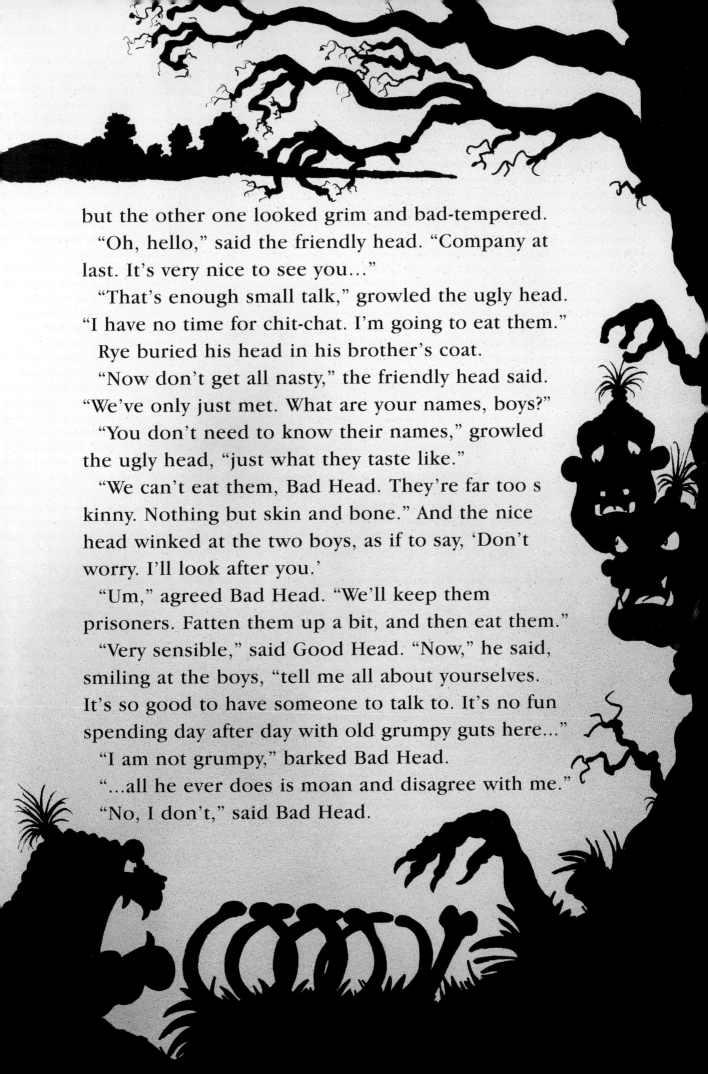

but the other one looked grim and bad-tempered.

"Oh, hello," said the friendly head. "Company at last. It's very nice to see you…"

"That's enough small talk," growled the ugly head. "I have no time for chit-chat. I'm going to eat them."

Rye buried his head in his brother's coat.

"Now don't get all nasty," the friendly head said. "We've only just met. What are your names, boys?"

"You don't need to know their names," growled the ugly head, "just what they taste like."

"We can't eat them, Bad Head. They're far too s kinny. Nothing but skin and bone." And the nice head winked at the two boys, as if to say, 'Don't worry. I'll look after you.'

"Um," agreed Bad Head. "We'll keep them prisoners. Fatten them up a bit, and then eat them."

"Very sensible," said Good Head. "Now," he said, smiling at the boys, "tell me all about yourselves. It's so good to have someone to talk to. It's no fun spending day after day with old grumpy guts here…"

"I am not grumpy," barked Bad Head.

"…all he ever does is moan and disagree with me."

"No, I don't," said Bad Head.

Good Head sat down next to the boys and asked them lots of questions. Where did they come from, why had they run away from home, and so on. The night wore on and the boys grew tired. Good Head was pleasant to talk to; he seemed to understand and was full of good advice. Bad Head just grumbled and muttered. At last Good Head fell asleep and left the boys alone with Bad Head. He turned to them with a nasty grin.

"I am going to eat you," he said. "I'm the fiercest monster in these parts. The fiercest monster anywhere in fact. If you've heard different, it's a fib."

And so he went on and on, making threats and being altogether very unpleasant. Eventually it was so late that the boys, scared though they were, could not keep their eyes open any longer. They fell into a deep sleep, with Bad Head still chuntering on in the darkness.

The boys awoke early the next morning to the sound of birdsong. In the morning sunshine, the monster didn't look anywhere near as frightening as it had the night before. Bad Head was snoring loudly, but Good Head was wide awake and smiling.

"Did you sleep well?" he whispered. "Sorry it's so uncomfortable. I have been meaning to build a little cabin or something, with comfy beds, but it's so hard to get anything done with Old Misery here. I could lead you back to the village, but he'll be awake soon, so we'll do it tonight."

And Good Head told the boys how he was going to save them. After a day in the forest, foraging for food to fatten up the boys, the monster would be very tired. When they sat down in the evening, the boys should sing a soothing lullaby. That would lull Bad Head to sleep and while he slept, Good Head would lead them to safety.

"Won't it make you sleepy, too?" asked Rye.

"You could put something in your ears," suggested Clay. "Then you won't hear us and you'll stay awake."

They all agreed that it was a good idea, but just then, Bad Head woke up.

"Is it morning already?" he grumbled. "I feel terrible. I'm cold and hungry."

They all spent a busy day in the forest, looking for food. Good Head showed them which berries and roots were safe to eat.

When evening fell, they sat beside a warm fire and talked. Good Head said that having to feed a few chickens wasn't such a bad thing if you had a warm house to live in and a soft bed, and the boys had to agree that the life they'd run away from wasn't so bad after all.

"What nonsense," grumbled Bad Head, rather sleepily.

Good Head winked at the boys; it was their sign to begin singing, while Good Head carefully rolled up some leaves and stuffed them into his ears.

The boys started to sing a lullaby:

"Rock a bye baby,
On the tree top.
When the wind blows,
The cradle will rock."

Bad Head's eyes closed for a moment and then jerked open again. "Rubbish," he muttered.

"When the bough breaks,
The cradle will fall.
Down will come baby,
Cradle and all."

It worked. Bad Head was fast asleep. He was lolling forward and snoring once more.
"Quickly," whispered Good Head.
They rose to their feet and hurried as fast, but as quietly as they could, out of the forest.

When they reached the edge the boys turned to Good Head.

"Thank you," they whispered.

"My pleasure," said Good Head. "Now hurry."

Clay and Rye scampered across the open fields towards home. After a little while, they stopped because they could hear voices.

"What's going on?" asked Bad Head.

"The boys," said Good Head. "They got away."

"They got away!" shouted Bad Head. "You useless monster. Why didn't you stop them?"

"They were too fast," said Good Head. "Anyway, you weren't a lot of help, snoring away…"

"What can we eat now?" grumbled Bad Head.

The voices faded away into the forest and the boys ran gratefully home. They would have some explaining to do when they got back, but then they would put the chickens away for the night and snuggle up thankfully into their own soft, cosy beds.

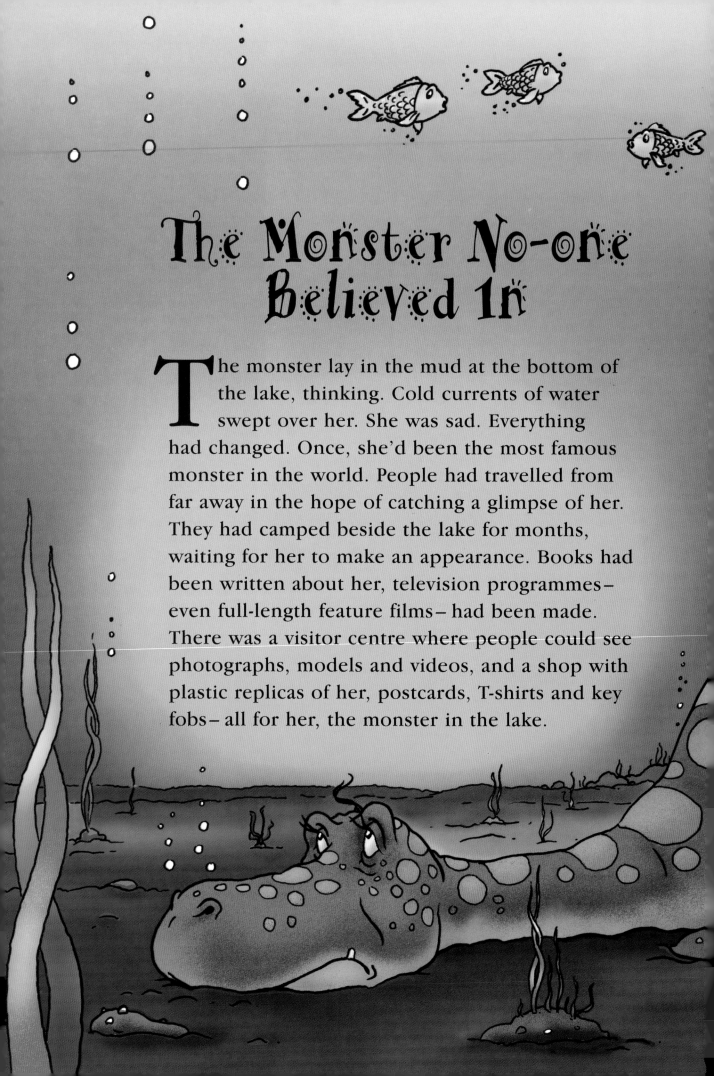

The Monster No-one Believed In

The monster lay in the mud at the bottom of the lake, thinking. Cold currents of water swept over her. She was sad. Everything had changed. Once, she'd been the most famous monster in the world. People had travelled from far away in the hope of catching a glimpse of her. They had camped beside the lake for months, waiting for her to make an appearance. Books had been written about her, television programmes— even full-length feature films— had been made. There was a visitor centre where people could see photographs, models and videos, and a shop with plastic replicas of her, postcards, T-shirts and key fobs— all for her, the monster in the lake.

But now the visitor centre was closed and few people bothered to stand around in the cold for a glimpse of her. What could have gone wrong?

She knew the answer: she'd been too mean with her appearances. Once every twenty years just wasn't enough. People had got bored and they'd gone off to pursue other monsters that showed themselves more often. They'd gone off to chase Bigfoot and measure corn circles.

She knew what to do. She had to rouse herself. Swim to the surface and make a splash.

"I'll just swim across the lake," she said to herself. "Show a couple of humps. No, let's make it a triple-humper, with a big wake. That's sure to get them all interested again."

She raised herself up rather stiffly, and swam over to the far shore.

"Here goes," she said.

She swam across the lake, propelling herself along with her powerful front flippers, her neck

outstretched, her legs trailing along behind her like tree-trunks, her big spotted back breaking the surface of the water. Nothing could make a wake like that, not an otter or a floating log or a big fish. She knew that when the people saw it, there'd be a frenzy of activity with cameras flashing and helicopters full of journalists. She'd be all over the papers the next day.

She lifted her neck out of the water and looked towards the shore. It was empty. There was no-one there. In the distance, she could see a campsite with lots of colourful tents. There were people there, but they weren't looking towards the lake. They were sitting outside their tents, reading newspapers and frying up sausages for supper. Others were playing football. No-one was interested in her.

The monster drifted sadly back to the bottom. It was no good; no-one believed in the monster in the lake any more.

The monster had liked fame, she enjoyed all the attention. Now she felt very alone and unwanted. There was only one thing to do: she'd have to show herself properly.

She swam to the shore. Then she lumbered across the grass towards the campsite. She felt heavy and awkward; she wasn't used to walking. She walked straight into the middle of the campsite and pulled herself up to her full height. A man in a deckchair looked up from his crossword.

"Ha, ha," he laughed. "That's great. Hey Ma, come out and look at this."

A woman walked out of the tent.

"Hey kids, that's a great costume," she cried. "Wherever did you get it?" The monster roared. "That's terrific," she said. "Sounds so realistic. Now have a wash. Supper'll be ready in just a few minutes."

'Oh no,' thought the monster. 'They think I'm children dressed up in a costume.'

She lumbered into the centre of the campsite where the children were playing football.

"Hey, great costume Dad," said the goalkeeper.

"You look just like a monster. But can you get off the pitch? We're in the middle of a game here." The children carried on playing, passing the ball around her and shouting, "Joke's over Dad. You're spoiling the game."

The monster walked sadly back to the lake. She slumped gloomily down by the water's edge, her neck hanging wearily. Just then she heard footsteps. She looked up to see a girl walking quietly along. The girl didn't see the monster until the last moment. But when she did, her eyes became as wide as saucers and she let out a scream.

"It's the monster!" she shrieked.

"Oh, I wouldn't bother yourself with all that," said the monster to the astonished little girl. "Nobody will take any notice."

"Wh-wh-why?" stammered the girl.

The monster explained that no-one believed in her any more – everyone thought she was just someone in a costume.

"My ten thousand years of fame is over," she said sadly. "I suppose it couldn't last forever."

"Well, I believe in you," said the girl. "We'll have to think of something that will get everyone's attention. I know – why don't I drift out onto the lake and pretend to be in trouble. Then you can rescue me. They always make a big fuss over someone who rescues a person. Then they'll see that you're the real monster and you'll make it into the headlines again."

The monster smiled. It was as good a plan as any. She slipped once again into the cold water. The little girl climbed into a boat and rowed herself expertly out onto the lake. Then she deliberately pushed the oars away.

"Help! HELP!" she cried, standing up in the boat and facing the campsite. The campers heard her and came running to the shore.

"Get another boat," cried someone.

"Ring the coastguard or the fire brigade," shouted another.

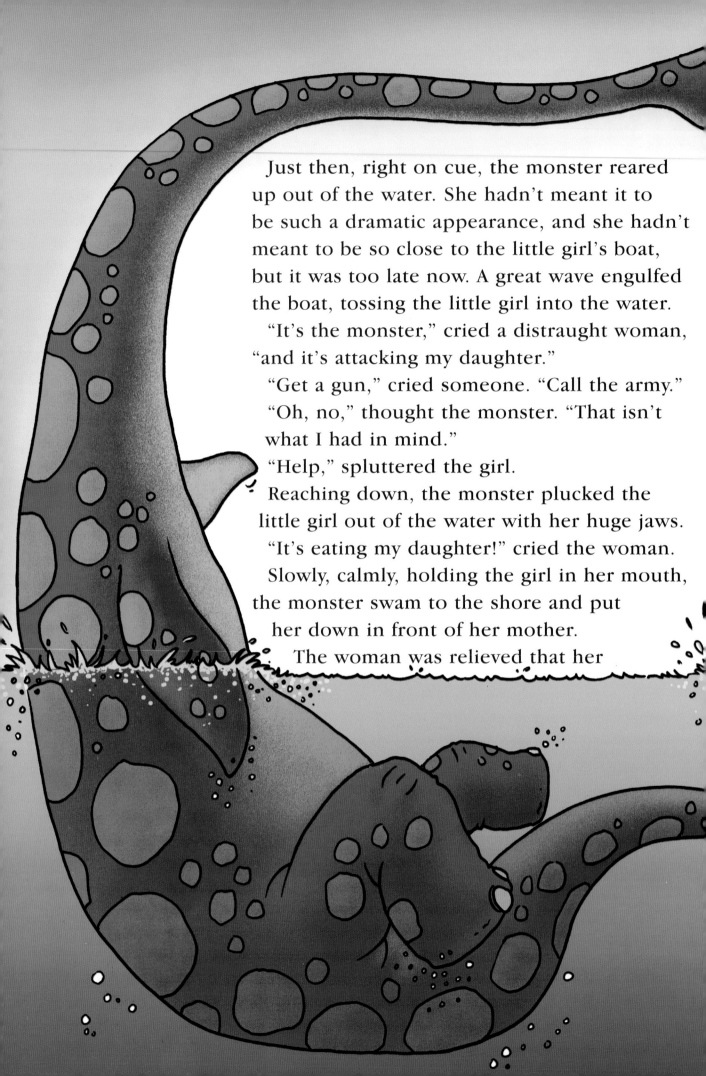

Just then, right on cue, the monster reared
up out of the water. She hadn't meant it to
be such a dramatic appearance, and she hadn't
meant to be so close to the little girl's boat,
but it was too late now. A great wave engulfed
the boat, tossing the little girl into the water.

"It's the monster," cried a distraught woman,
"and it's attacking my daughter."

"Get a gun," cried someone. "Call the army."

"Oh, no," thought the monster. "That isn't
what I had in mind."

"Help," spluttered the girl.

Reaching down, the monster plucked the
little girl out of the water with her huge jaws.

"It's eating my daughter!" cried the woman.

Slowly, calmly, holding the girl in her mouth,
the monster swam to the shore and put
her down in front of her mother.

The woman was relieved that her

daughter was safe and her cries changed to "The monster's saved my daughter."

Everyone took up the cry. "The monster saved the girl," they cried. "The monster's a hero." Cameras were flashing, video cameras whirred and the monster could hear the steady chop, chop, chop of a helicopter as it approached.

'I think that's enough for me,' she thought. 'I'm off.' She turned gracefully and dived, down to the bottom of her lake, leaving the excited campers on the shore still cheering and shouting and reaching frantically for their cameras and mobile phones.

The monster sank into the mud at the bottom of the lake. 'I think I'll lay low for a while,' she thought. 'Just for another 20 years or so. A monster can only take so much attention, after all.'

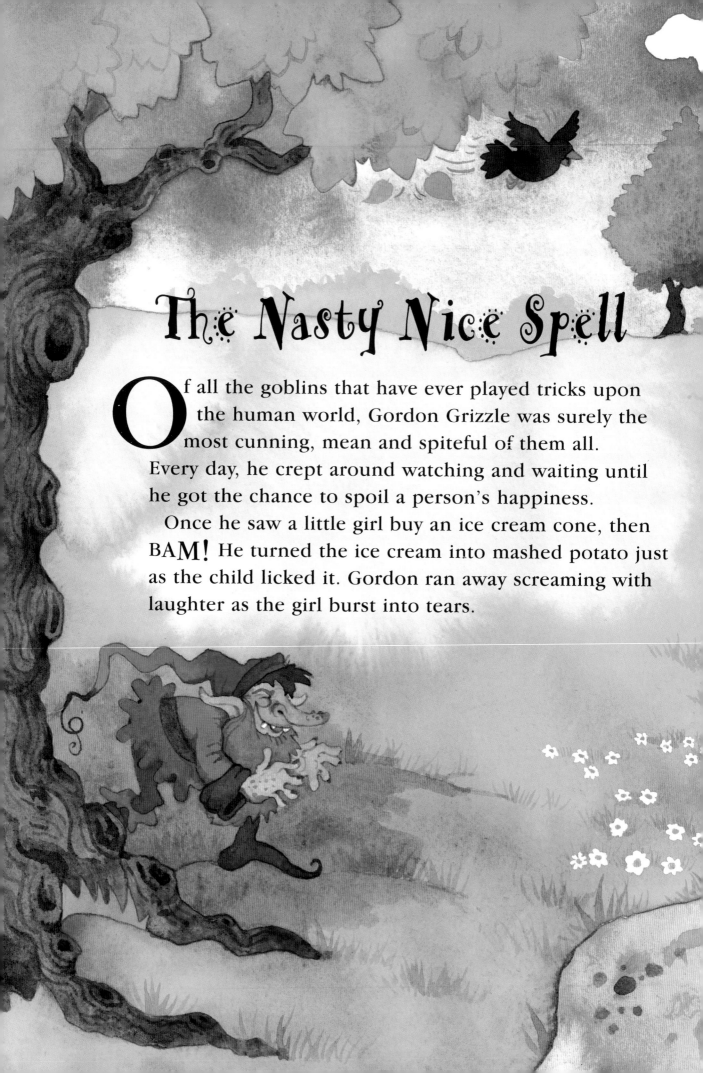

The Nasty Nice Spell

Of all the goblins that have ever played tricks upon the human world, Gordon Grizzle was surely the most cunning, mean and spiteful of them all. Every day, he crept around watching and waiting until he got the chance to spoil a person's happiness.

Once he saw a little girl buy an ice cream cone, then **BAM!** He turned the ice cream into mashed potato just as the child licked it. Gordon ran away screaming with laughter as the girl burst into tears.

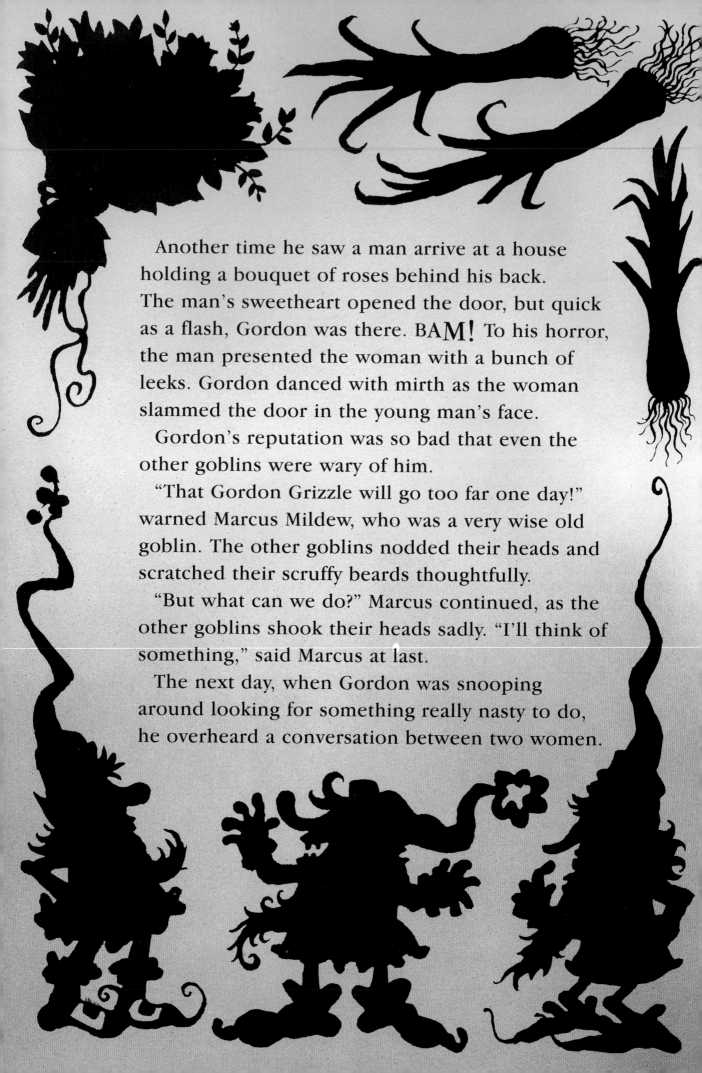

Another time he saw a man arrive at a house holding a bouquet of roses behind his back. The man's sweetheart opened the door, but quick as a flash, Gordon was there. BAM! To his horror, the man presented the woman with a bunch of leeks. Gordon danced with mirth as the woman slammed the door in the young man's face.

Gordon's reputation was so bad that even the other goblins were wary of him.

"That Gordon Grizzle will go too far one day!" warned Marcus Mildew, who was a very wise old goblin. The other goblins nodded their heads and scratched their scruffy beards thoughtfully.

"But what can we do?" Marcus continued, as the other goblins shook their heads sadly. "I'll think of something," said Marcus at last.

The next day, when Gordon was snooping around looking for something really nasty to do, he overheard a conversation between two women.

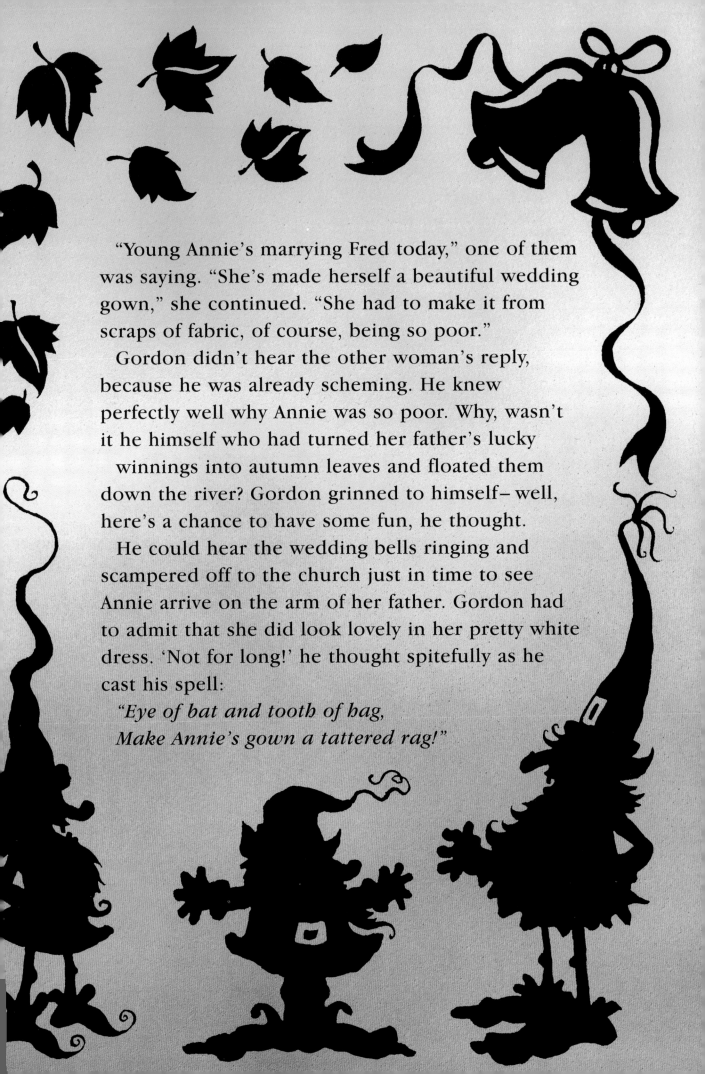

"Young Annie's marrying Fred today," one of them was saying. "She's made herself a beautiful wedding gown," she continued. "She had to make it from scraps of fabric, of course, being so poor."

Gordon didn't hear the other woman's reply, because he was already scheming. He knew perfectly well why Annie was so poor. Why, wasn't it he himself who had turned her father's lucky winnings into autumn leaves and floated them down the river? Gordon grinned to himself– well, here's a chance to have some fun, he thought.

He could hear the wedding bells ringing and scampered off to the church just in time to see Annie arrive on the arm of her father. Gordon had to admit that she did look lovely in her pretty white dress. 'Not for long!' he thought spitefully as he cast his spell:

"Eye of bat and tooth of hag,
Make Annie's gown a tattered rag!"

BAM! The deed was done. Gordon giggled to himself. He didn't even bother to look back as he slipped in through the church door. He heard the wedding guests gasp as they turned to look at Annie. "Ha, ha, ha – I bet she looks truly awful," he sneered. "Now let's see to the groom!"

"Slimy slugs and all things naughty,
Make Fred's face look old and warty!"

BAM! There was another gasp from the people as they turned round to stare at the groom. Annie's jaw dropped in amazement.

Gordon peeped out from behind a pew. To his utter astonishment, there stood Annie in the most gorgeous silver gown that he had ever seen. A beautiful diamond tiara held her veil in place, and Gordon could see her eyes fill with tears as she smiled at Fred.

"Oh, Fred!" she breathed. "You look so… different."

Gordon spun around to look at Fred. He looked not old and warty but younger and more handsome!

What's more, he was impeccably dressed in a suit of rich velveteen. Gordon was livid. This wasn't what he had intended to happen! The young couple looked happier than ever and that wouldn't do at all. He shook his fists and stamped his feet with rage. Then he began to realise something. He was jealous.

"It's not fair," he wailed to himself. "I want to be happy, too!" Soon he cast another spell:

"Banana skins and custard pies,
Make me happy, healthy, truthful and wise!"

'That's better!' thought Gordon, skipping out of the church, though he didn't actually feel any better. In fact, he felt much worse.

'Ah, I know what I forgot!' he thought:

"Dragon's toe and ogre's head,
Make me young and handsome – just like Fred!"

Now, he felt really very peculiar. He seemed to be shrinking and looking down, he saw to his horror that in place of his leather boots was a pair of slimy, green, webbed feet. Gordon realised that he had turned into a toad!

"That'll teach you!" said a familiar voice from high up. It was Marcus Mildew, but Gordon could barely see him over the top of his highly polished shoes.

"I've been watching you, Gordon," said Marcus. "I've seen your spiteful ways, spoiling everyone's fun. So I decided to spoil your fun, too! From now on, every time you cast a bad spell you'll find the opposite happens. And you're going to remain a toad until someone shows you some kindness." And with that, Marcus was gone.

Gordon stared at his long, wet toes. Now he understood why all his spells were going wrong. What had he asked for? To be happy, healthy and wise – and handsome! And now he was the opposite of all of these. Oh dear! He really felt very sorry for himself.

There was no time to dwell upon his misfortunes, however, for the world was now a very dangerous place. A pair of yellow eyes loomed towards him – a cat! Gordon sprang high into the air just as the cat pounced, narrowly missing him with its sharp claws.

'I'm feeling parched. I must get to water,' thought Gordon, though he had no idea which way to turn. The trouble was, being so small, everything looked different. He looked through a sea of legs and feet on the pavement.

'I'm sure there's a stream on the other side of the road,' he thought. Dodging the feet, he hopped his way to the edge of the pavement, and was nearly squashed flat several times. Monstrous cars

Now, he felt really very peculiar. He seemed to be shrinking and looking down, he saw to his horror that in place of his leather boots was a pair of slimy, green, webbed feet. Gordon realised that he had turned into a toad!

"That'll teach you!" said a familiar voice from high up. It was Marcus Mildew, but Gordon could barely see him over the top of his highly polished shoes.

"I've been watching you, Gordon," said Marcus. "I've seen your spiteful ways, spoiling everyone's fun. So I decided to spoil your fun, too! From now on, every time you cast a bad spell you'll find the opposite happens. And you're going to remain a toad until someone shows you some kindness." And with that, Marcus was gone.

Gordon stared at his long, wet toes. Now he understood why all his spells were going wrong. What had he asked for? To be happy, healthy and wise – and handsome! And now he was the opposite of all of these. Oh dear! He really felt very sorry for himself.

There was no time to dwell upon his misfortunes, however, for the world was now a very dangerous place. A pair of yellow eyes loomed towards him – a cat! Gordon sprang high into the air just as the cat pounced, narrowly missing him with its sharp claws.

'I'm feeling parched. I must get to water,' thought Gordon, though he had no idea which way to turn. The trouble was, being so small, everything looked different. He looked through a sea of legs and feet on the pavement.

'I'm sure there's a stream on the other side of the road,' he thought. Dodging the feet, he hopped his way to the edge of the pavement, and was nearly squashed flat several times. Monstrous cars

roared past and Gordon was too petrified to cross the road. Then he spotted a boy pointing at him.

'I hope he's going to show me kindness,' thought Gordon, quaking with fear. To his horror, though, he saw the boy pick up a stone. The boy raised his arm to hurl the missile and Gordon closed his eyes in fright.

"Stop!" called a voice. Gordon opened his eyes to see Fred scolding the boy. Then he knelt down and gently picked Gordon up. "Let's take this poor toad back to our garden, Annie," said Fred.

Soon Gordon was sitting on a lily leaf in the middle of Fred's pond, watching all the wedding guests having a party. He looked at his reflection in the water – and looked again. He was a goblin again! Without thinking, he dived in and swam to the edge of the pond.

What a sorry sight Gordon was as he crept home with his clothes dripping and stinking, and covered in slimy duckweed. But I think he'd learned his lesson, don't you?